About Simon Says: Mine

Mountain Masters & Dark Haven: Book 2

Once again dynamic author Cherise Sinclair creates a magnificent and deliciously rendered story that captures the heart and soul, captivating the reader. The characters have a great emotional depth, courage and passion combined they support an outstanding story. The plotting is exquisite with the thrilling action, dialogue and well-crafted characters that are so enchanting that they will make the reader's heart race in anticipation of each new delightful and erotic scene.

~ The Romance Studio

With an empty nest and divorce in hand, Rona decides it's time to explore the fantasies that nourished her through a long, tedious marriage to a man whose idea of outrageous sex was leaving the lights on. At the top of her fantasy list is touring Dark Haven, the BDSM club, but she isn't prepared for the effect of a powerful Dom. When Master Simon takes control and introduces her to toys and sensations she's never felt before, she realizes he could fulfill every fantasy on her list all by himself. But she's vowed to never get trapped in a relationship again.

One of the most popular Doms in Dark Haven, Master Simon has had his fill of eager, shallow, young subs. Rona is older, intelligent, independent…and sweetly submissive. After an evening of intense pleasure and despite her obvious attraction, she refuses to see him again. He needs a way to change her mind. She's not the first sub he's taken on a journey of exploration, but he's beginning to think she might be the last.

Master Simon is one of the more popular Doms at Dark Haven and he holds the key to my heart. I loved how he handled Rona, a more tentative and older submissive. They are such a pair and Sinclair gives them a story that is definitely worth checking out.

~ Under the Covers Book Blog

Want to be notified of the next release?

Sent only on release day, Cherise's newsletters contain freebies,
excerpts, and articles.
Sign up at:
www.CheriseSinclair.com/NewsletterForm

Simon Says: Mine

Mountain Masters & Dark Haven: 2

Cherise Sinclair

VanScoy Publishing Group

Simon Says: Mine

Copyright © 2010 by Cherise Sinclair
Print Edition
ISBN 978-0-9861195-4-5
Published by VanScoy Publishing Group
Cover Artist: Hot Damn Designs
~ Reprint ~
~ Originally published in the anthology, Doms of Dark Haven ~

Author's Note

To my readers,

The books I write are fiction, not reality, and as in most romantic fiction, the romance is compressed into a very, very short time period.

You, my darlings, live in the real world, and I want you to take a little more time in your relationships. Good Doms don't grow on trees, and there are some strange people out there. So while you're looking for that special Dom, please, be careful.

When you find him, realize he can't read your mind. Yes, frightening as it might be, you're going to have to open up and talk to him. And you listen to him, in return. Share your hopes and fears, what you want from him, what scares you spitless. Okay, he may try to push your boundaries a little—he's a Dom, after all—but you will have your safe word. You will have a safe word, am I clear? Use protection. Have a back-up person. Communicate.

Remember: safe, sane, and consensual.

Know that I'm hoping you find that special, loving person who will understand your needs and hold you close.

And while you're looking or even if you have already found your dearheart, come and hang out with the Doms in Dark Haven.

Love,
Cherise

Chapter One

*S*OMEONE *SHOULD LOCK me up in the psych unit.* Rona McGregor sucked in a breath of cool night air. Visiting a BDSM club held third place on her fantasy list, but she'd decided to take it out of order. Just this once. With an eager smile and her heart pounding, she lifted her ankle-length skirt and shoved open the door to the notorious San Francisco club named Dark Haven.

She hadn't done anything remotely adventurous in the last twenty years, but her time for insanity had finally arrived. Her children were in college. No husband anymore—*thank you, God.* She'd lost weight—she glanced down at her very full bodice—well, *some* weight. But truly, she didn't look too bad for a woman on the downslide to forty.

Rather than the den of sin Rona had expected, the small entry was dismally bland. A handful of people, also dressed in nineteenth-century clothing, stood in line to give their entrance fees to the woman behind the desk. A few minutes later Rona reached the front.

The perky young woman beamed at her. "Hi. Welcome to Dark Haven's Victorian night. Members sign in here." The receptionist's purple gown matched the streaks in her spiked hair. She'd apparently ripped out the bodice, leaving only pink netting over her breasts.

Rona suppressed a snort of laughter. Maybe the place wasn't all that bland. After her years as a nurse, bare breasts didn't unsettle her, but she'd never seen any quite so vividly displayed before. "I'm not a member."

"No problem. Oh, hey, I love your outfit. Major authentic. Did you go to the Dickens Faire at the Cow Palace today?"

Rona nodded. "That's where I found out about this theme night." And it had seemed like a sign from heaven. There she'd been, already in the perfect attire. "Since I haven't been in a place like this before, is there anything I should know?"

"Nah. Here's a membership form and release. Fill it out and give me twenty bucks to get in and five more for the membership, and you're good to go." The receptionist pushed a clipboard of papers across the desk. "If you hurry, you'll catch Master Simon giving an erotic flogging demo."

"Master Simon?" A young woman in the line squealed. "Oh God, he's so hot!" She waved her hand in front of her face so vigorously that Rona almost offered the lace fan clipped to her waistband.

Rona filled out the forms and eyed the others signing in. Satisfaction eased her nerves at the sight of the costumes: an evening gown over wide hoops, a tea gown like hers, two maid outfits with aprons. Any other night she'd be clueless as to what to wear to a BDSM club, but tonight she fit right in. How could she have resisted?

Then she noticed one lady wearing only a chemise. Another woman removed her coat, revealing a pristine white apron—and nothing else. A small worm of unease squirmed in Rona's stomach. She gave the receptionist the paperwork and asked, "Am I a little overdressed?"

"Hell no." The girl put the money away and handed over a membership card. "Dommes wear that much, and lots of subs start off dressed. Makes it more interesting when you have to strip, right?"

Strip. In a bar? Me? She'd only planned on watching. The

thought of actually participating sent a shiver of excitement up her spine. "Right."

Rona tucked the card into her reticule, smoothed her gown, then opened the door to the inner sanctum and stepped into the nineteenth century. Her startled breath of air was redolent with perfumes, leather, sweat, and sex. As the passionate sound of Grieg's Piano Concerto in A Minor surrounded her, she moved into the dimly lit room crowded with men in frock coats and women in bell-like gowns. *How fun.*

She walked forward slowly, trying not to gawk. Dark wood tables and chairs dotted the center of the long room. A small dance floor took up one corner in the far back; a shiny metal bar with two bartenders behind it occupied the other. All fairly normal. Where'd they hide the kinky stuff that her erotic romance novels had promised?

Then a man strolled past wearing nothing except a terrifying harness strapped to his cock and balls. Rona's mouth dropped. *Crom*, but she could almost feel her nonexistent male equipment shrivel up in horror.

Shaking her head, she started toward the bar, then noticed the right and left wall each held a small stage.

One platform stood empty. On the other... Rona took an involuntary step back, bumped into someone, and muttered an apology without looking away from the stage where—*surely that's illegal*—a man was whipping a woman chained to a post.

BDSM. Remember, Rona? She'd read about whips and chains and stuff—but seeing it? *Whoa.*

She pressed a hand to her hammering heart and squashed the impulse to go and snatch the whip from him. As if she could anyway. He stood a good six feet tall with a mature man's solid build; she had a feeling that if someone were to punch him, he'd just absorb it. In keeping with the night's theme, he wore a green silk vest over an old-fashioned white shirt. The rolled-up sleeves displayed thickly muscled forearms.

In contrast, his victim was completely naked, her dusky skin glowing dark red from the effects of the whip—No, it was called a flogger, right? The multiple strands stroked up and down her back so evenly that Rona could time her breathing to the rhythm. Mesmerized, she moved closer—threading her way through the tables and chairs scattered around the stage—and chose a table near the front.

Flogging. The word sounded brutal, but this…this was almost beautiful. The man swung the flogger in a figure-eight pattern, hitting one side of the woman, then the other. Rona leaned forward, setting her elbows on the table. He never struck over the brunette's spine or flanks, obviously avoiding her kidneys with appallingly impressive skill.

He slowed and paused for a moment before whispering the strands across the woman's back and legs. The woman had her side to the audience, and Rona could see her flushed face and glazed eyes. She was panting from the pain or… The victim's bottom tilted outward, swaying in a way that implied arousal, not pain.

Arousal.

A grin flashed over the man's tanned face. He stroked the woman's inner thighs with the leather strands, up and down, each time moving closer to the V between her legs. She moaned and wiggled.

Rona inhaled slowly, trying to damp the excitement sizzling through her veins.

The man started the flogging again, down the woman's back, bottom, and thighs. Suddenly, he altered the pattern and flicked the lashes between her legs, right onto her pussy. The woman gasped.

So did Rona. She'd been so immersed, it felt as if the whip had hit her…there. Her insides melted into a puddle of liquid heat. The receptionist had had it right—this was an *erotic* flogging. *Whew.*

The music changed, beginning the dramatic conclusion of the movement, and even the murmured conversations died. Rona could almost smell the arousal in the room, and her hands clenched. *So violent…so exciting.*

He was flogging the woman's thighs now, the blows gradually moving upward, even harder than before. And again he slapped the strands lightly between her legs. The woman's squeak turned into a low moan. Then her back, down her thighs, and up slowly. The third time he hit her pussy, the woman shriek and climaxed, writhing in her chains.

A trickle of sweat ran down the hollow at the base of Rona's spine, and her ragged breathing fought against the tight corset. How could something like this—a whipping—make her so hot?

The crowd cheered as the man released his victim. Although *victim* couldn't be the right word, not with that satisfied expression on her face. Rona blinked in surprise when a younger man jumped onto the stage and took the woman into his arms. After a very tongue-laden kiss, the couple stopped long enough for the two men to shake hands and for the woman to kiss the back of the flogger's hand.

He'd whipped a woman who wasn't his?

Rona swallowed. Her fantasy of a lover tying her down, maybe even spanking her, seemed pallid next to the reality of what had just occurred.

Across the room, a man and woman began to set up equipment on the empty platform. As the music changed to Nine Inch Nails, the crowd divided: some to the other stage, some to the dance floor. Left alone, the man who'd done the flogging wiped down the post and packed his weapon into a leather bag. Hefting the bag over his shoulder, he strode toward the stage steps and halted at the edge, stopped by a small covey of—Rona snorted—groupies? Did BDSM have groupies?

Shaking her head in bemusement, she turned to look for a waitress. Maybe she should add "Try out a hot dom" to her list. She grinned. Her ex had always ridiculed her five-year goal plans—as if disorganization were better. He'd have had heart failure if he'd seen her fantasy list.

No waitress in sight. She returned her attention to the stage and sighed in disappointment. Empty, like many of the chairs around her. Most of the people had moved to the other side.

A *thump* drew her attention to the table next to hers, and she gaped like a moron. The man from the stage stood there with his leather bag at his feet. On the table lay a black frock coat and old-fashioned cuff links that he must have removed before starting his demonstration.

She watched as he rolled down the sleeves of his shirt. His dark eyes looked almost black, and his deeply tanned face was lean and hard. With the lines of pain and laughter around his mouth and eyes, and silver glinting in his neatly trimmed black hair, he must have been around forty. And yet when he moved, muscles rippled and strained the shoulders of his white shirt.

Not only a hunk, but older than her. Yet she didn't even consider flirting. Not with this one. He was too…too intimidating. Not like a young, buff underwear model, all gorgeous and everything, but in a far-more-dangerous way.

Of course he's dangerous—he has a flogger, and he knows how to use it.

All her minuscule experience with BDSM came from reading erotic romances. She'd always wanted to try a few things, but Mark had laughed at her and refused to do anything to liven up their sex life. Not that they'd even had a sex life the last few years.

Her horizons had definitely expanded since the divorce, but not enough for her to jump into seriously kinky stuff. She'd simply planned to watch and note some ideas to add to her fantasy list, but certainly not to make a pass at a really, really experienced BDSM practitioner.

No matter how gorgeous he looked.

Don't drool. She tried to casually lean back but slouching in a corset was impossible. Stymied, she turned her gaze to the other stage, where a woman costumed as a schoolmarm wrapped ropes around a young man wearing only breeches. Rona managed to keep her attention there for, oh, a good minute, before returning to the man.

She frowned. He was trying to get a cuff link into his shirt and failing miserably. For some reason, the fingers of his left hand didn't bend. His frustrated growl switched him in her mind from a hunk to someone who needed her.

She walked over, pushed his hand to one side, and fastened the heavy silver link. "There." With a smile, she patted his arm comfortingly. "Now—"

She looked up into intent, powerful eyes, and every cell in her body went into a meltdown. He kept her pinned with those dark eyes, studying her as if he could see through to her soul.

He moved closer, forcing her to tilt her head back to look up at him. When her breath stuck in her chest, his lips curved into a faint smile. "You didn't even think before coming to my rescue, did you?" he asked, and his voice was as dark and smooth as everything else about him.

She should apologize. "I-I'm—"

"Be silent."

Her throat just plain shut down completely, and the laugh lines around his eyes crinkled slightly. "Submissive," he murmured. "But no submissive would shove a master's hands away and take over. You're new?"

He didn't wait for an answer but ran a finger down her cheek, her neck, across the tops of her pushed-up breasts.

His touch burned through her, leaving an aching need. The trembling inside her stomach worked outward until her legs wobbled. "Please," she whispered.

He tilted his head. "Please what, pet?"

"Please don't tease me." Feeling like an idiot—a very confused, aroused idiot—she dropped her gaze and tried to take a step back.

His hand closed around her upper arm, firmly enough that she knew she'd go nowhere.

"Look at me." A finger under her chin raised her face. His lips curved into a faint smile. "Very new, I see."

"Yes." Her next effort to move back met the same results—none.

"A submissive need not call any dom but her own 'Sir,' but if she approaches a dom on her own and then reacts like this"—his finger left her chin to stroke over her trembling lips—"then she had best address that dom as 'Sir.'"

Acutely aware of the warmth of his finger still on her lips, she felt as if she were drowning in molten air.

He paused, then prompted, "Say, 'Yes, Sir.'"

Oh. "Yes, Sir." She'd used the phrase before, teasingly with the hospital doctors, sarcastically with idiots, but now it reverberated through her like the sound of a bass drum.

"Very good."

A woman wearing only a corset, fishnet stockings, and high heels suddenly dropped to her knees beside the table. "Master Simon. Can I serve you in any way?"

He turned.

Freed from his gaze, Rona tried to retreat, but his hand, hard and ruthless, tightened. The feeling of being controlled swamped her senses.

Her heart raced as if she'd received an injection of Adrenalin, but with his attention diverted, she managed to pull in a steadying breath. *I'm a mature woman, an administrator, smart and professional. Why do I feel like a cornered mouse?* And it turned her on like someone had opened a hormone faucet.

She glanced down at the kneeling woman and winced. Not only willing to give Master Simon anything he wanted, but also blonde, slender, gorgeous. And young.

Rona was none of those. *Escape. Definitely time to escape.*

"THANK YOU, NO," Simon told the kneeling sub, waving her off politely but firmly. Another youngster. He smothered a sigh. The enthusiastic, young ones seemed so very undeveloped. He preferred *women*, yet the interesting, older subs were usually involved, or they had emotional problems. He hadn't met a well-balanced submissive in quite some time.

I'm lonely. Divorced for several years, his son in college, his house empty, he'd recently grown aware of how much he'd like someone to embrace at night, to talk with in the evenings, to share everything from a new dessert to the day's victories and disasters. He could find a willing body all too easily, but not an open heart, an interesting mind, and an independent spirit.

But this one... Simon turned his attention to the submissive who'd dared to help him without asking. Not young, probably somewhere in her thirties. Her face had lines that said she'd seen sorrow. Had laughed. Her full breasts, pushed high and taut, displayed the silver striations that showed some baby had been held against her heart and nourished. The way she'd briskly brushed away his hands from the cuff told him she was used to being in charge. The melting look in her eyes when he'd touched her said she was submissive.

Very appealing. And oddly familiar. Had she visited the club before?

But she kept trying to retreat. *Why?* Of course, a dom might make an inexperienced sub nervous, but she'd shown definite interest before...before the interruption. His eyes narrowed. The kneeling sub had been young and pretty. Was this confident woman uncertain of her appeal?

She tugged at her arm again and actually frowned at him.

"I don't believe we finished our conversation," Simon said.

Her gaze lifted. In the dim bar, her eyes appeared blue or green. Her hair, a streaky color between blonde and brown, had been pulled back into an ugly Victorian bun. That would be the first thing he'd fix.

He held out his free hand. "My name is Simon."

As wary as a treed cat, she still managed to say politely, "It's nice to meet you, Simon."

That lovely, low voice would deepen after she came a few

times. His fingers closed over hers, and he kept his other hand wrapped around her arm. Now he had her securely trapped, and the knowledge appeared in her eyes. Her breath quickened, her tongue flicked over her lips, and she swayed, almost imperceptibly, toward him. Yes, the feeling of being controlled aroused her.

Now, wouldn't she look lovely in ropes? "And you are...?" he prompted.

"Rona."

"Scottish? Yes, it suits you." He looked down into her eyes, enjoying the slight tremble of her fingers in his. "Is this your first time in a BDSM club, Rona?"

"Yes."

"And how long have you been here?"

"Not even an hour."

"*Not even.*" The phrasing implied she felt off balance. And he'd definitely pushed—was still pushing, which wasn't appropriate or honorable to do to a sweet newbie. When he opened his hands and released her, the sense of loss surprised him. *I want to keep this one.*

But the choices, always, belonged to the submissive—unless and until she freely gave over those choices to him. "Do you want a guide, or would you rather explore on your own?"

She hesitated. "Um. Well..."

She didn't want a guide. Despite her obvious attraction to him, she'd prefer to see the place on her own. He almost laughed at his annoyance. Getting too accustomed to adulation, was he? This woman might tremble, but she wouldn't throw herself at anyone's feet, and that only increased his interest.

"All right." He ran a finger down her cheek, marking her as his in the indefinable way of dominance. "I will see you later, then."

As Master Simon walked away with an easy, confident stride, Rona stared after him. He'd only touched her with a finger, and her pulse had increased to serious tachycardia.

She'd read BDSM books but hadn't really grasped the power a

dominant could exert. That walking, talking model of intimidation had wielded his eyes and his…his sheer presence…as skillfully as he'd used that flogger. Lord help her.

After sucking in a breath, she shook her head, told her body to stop reacting, and headed for the bar. One bottled water coming right up.

The diversion and the icy water worked, and within a few minutes, her self-possession returned. Putting her back to the bar, she looked around.

Lots of people, but no Master Simon in sight. Disappointment washed through her, cooler than the ice water. And how stupid to be disappointed after having turned him down. But she'd done the right thing. He was just too, too much,—her bottle stopped halfway to her mouth—and she'd totally chickened out, hadn't she? Here she'd made all those resolutions to dump her Miss Propriety image, to let go of her I'm-a-mother-and-a-wife-and-not-a-sensual-woman thinking, yet when a stunning man showed his interest, she'd run for the proverbial hills.

Of course, her plan for an exciting life hadn't included hanging out with a guy who enjoyed multitailed whips, but still…

She'd do better next time. For now, she needed to scope out the place. Aside from the demonstrations on the stages, she hadn't spotted any of the "scenes" she'd read about. But people kept disappearing down stairs near the front, so maybe the fun stuff happened on the lower level. She picked up her bottle and eased past a group of people, including a black-haired woman wearing a cute pink and white corset. Rona noticed the bright pink streaks in the woman's hair and grinned, remembering the receptionist. Matching hair color to clothing—not exactly correct for the period.

At the bottom of the stairs, she stopped, feeling as if she'd descended into a literal hell. Holy crap, Batman, but some of these people needed a psych eval. Like the blonde letting a guy stick needles into her breasts. In pure reflex, Rona crossed her arms over her chest when the man shoved another needle in, right through the woman's nipple.

Now that was just wrong. Maybe she should go back to the car and get her first-aid kit.

Instead she walked farther into the room. The industrial Goth music from upstairs blended with the sounds of flesh being struck, moans, high cries, the *snap* of a whip, a long, shuddering groan. A series of cracking noises sounded way too close, and she jumped, looked around, and then snorted a laugh. She'd clenched her water bottle so hard that the plastic had crumpled. Noisily.

She rolled her eyes. Hopefully no one would yell *boo*! at her, or she'd go into cardiac arrest.

By the second scene area, she noticed guys scoping her out. Cool. She moved her hips and made her full skirts sway. *Sexy me.* Then a young woman walked past clad in only a G-string, all firm skin and high breasts. Right. *Sexy me as long as I'm wearing clothes.* She might have lost some weight and firmed things up a bit, but those things were still well over thirty years old.

An hour or so later she knew a heck of a lot more about what kinky people did for fun. Watching Simon's flogging demonstration hadn't prepared her for canes or black whips—although no one in the place came close to his skill—let alone hot wax, needles, gags, and masks. As one dominant applied a line of small suction cups up a woman's back, Rona wondered if the glass cups ever went on more…intimate spots. She mentally added it to the list of things to try—someday—and just the thought sent a zip of excitement right to her clit.

As if she weren't already excited. A few steps farther, she glanced through a large window into a very authentic-looking medieval dungeon. A black-haired woman was manacled to the stone wall, and a man in jeans slapped the poor woman between the legs, sending her right up onto her toes. A minute later he dropped to his knees, gripped her buttocks, and put his mouth on her pussy.

Rona swallowed and fanned her overheated face as she moved away. Shocking and erotic as heck.

By the time she'd toured the room, her corset bones felt like bony fingers digging into her ribs, and her clothes as if they weighed a good twenty pounds. Finding an empty couch, she collapsed onto it. *Oops.* Proper Victorian ladies didn't drop like rocks; they undoubtedly sank gracefully down to a seat and, of course, sat erect rather than leaning back.

She'd have made a lousy Victorian lady.

She'd probably make a lousy BDSM person too. In fact, she might not even like doing it, although watching stuff like the way that belt had hit the woman's round bottom made her really…warm.

Maybe, while here, she could try a little bit—just a taste, not a whole meal. Have someone tie her hands or something. A quiver trickled through her insides at the thought of actually acting out some of her fantasies.

Mouth suddenly dry, she sipped the last of her lukewarm water. First she'd have to meet a dom. She could watch another demonstration. But the shows—scenes—down here seemed more personal. More intimate. If Simon wanted to beat on her, she'd rather do it here than upstairs.

She choked on the water. What the heck had brought Simon back to mind?

Well, she knew the answer to that. Any woman would want him, with that devastating combination of easy manners and merciless authority. *And don't think about his voice*—as smooth and rich as Dove's dark chocolate. Goose bumps prickled up her arms, and she sighed.

Hopeless, she was just hopeless. And *Master* Simon was way out of her league. She needed someone less intimidating.

She looked around. *Hmmm.* Not the old guy over there or the fat one. She checked the other direction and spotted a tall blond, maybe in his late twenties. Rather cute. He stood with his hands behind his back, watching a nearby scene. When he looked around, his gaze met Rona's. She smiled at him. *You. Yeah, you. C'mere, honey.*

He blinked and headed over. "Hi. You're new here?"

"That's right."

Chapter Two

THERE YOU ARE. Simon stopped at the sight of the woman he'd been hunting. Someone else had captured his quarry first and secured her arms to chains dangling from the low suspension beam. The dom, one of the younger men, had removed her gown and petticoats, leaving her in a corset, sleeveless chemise, and drawers.

What a nice picture. Lovely, soft curves and pale skin, big eyes and a stubborn chin.

However, for someone so thoroughly restrained, the submissive had taken control of the play.

"Pitiful," Xavier said, joining him. The owner of Dark Haven wore a frock coat like Simon's over a silver-and-blue paisley vest. Very dapper, especially with his black hair braided back almost to his ass.

Simon raised an eyebrow at his friend. "You know the sub?"

"No. She's not been here before."

Then why is she so familiar? Simon watched for a moment and winced when Rona laughed at the dom. True, she had an adorable, low laugh, but the dom had totally lost control of the scene. From the young man's unhappy expression, he didn't know how to get it back—if he'd ever had it. The term "*submissive*" didn't necessarily mean pushover.

"I told David to stick to the easy subs," Xavier said.

"Friend of yours?"

"He took one of my classes for dominants. He's not bad, just inexperienced." Xavier started toward the scene, but a barmaid stopped him, chattering about a problem. He held up his hand to pause her, then turned to Simon. "Do me a favor and rescue David, would you? I'll join you shortly."

Simon heard Rona order the dom to try something in his bag and grinned. "She's a bossy one."

Xavier's black brows rose. "Like her, do you? Perhaps I won't owe you a favor after all."

"No, my friend, I will owe you one. However, since she's new to the lifestyle and community, I'd appreciate a reference." Simon clapped his shoulder and moved to where he could be seen but not interfere if David chose to ignore him. Not that there was any scene dynamic to destroy here.

David looked confused when he saw Simon, but he walked over. Frustration had tensed his muscles and jawline. "It's Simon, right?"

"Xavier sent me in case you wanted out. I met the sub earlier, and I wouldn't mind working with her."

"Hell yes. Take her." The dom scowled. "Xavier warned me about getting in over my head. Now I know what he meant."

"Like anything else, it takes practice. Does she have any hard limits or requests?"

"No blood sports. No anal. She wanted to play the rest by ear and chose 'Houston' for a safe word."

"As in 'Houston, we have a problem'?"

David grinned. "Yep."

She definitely has a sense of humor. Simon nodded acknowledgment and turned his attention to Rona, his anticipation rising. He'd wanted this woman since the minute she touched him. Totally illogical, but in life, as in the martial arts, he'd learned his instincts were rarely wrong.

He heard David grab his toy bag and leave, but didn't take his focus from the sub. He'd caught her as handily as any of the animals he'd hunted in his youth.

She'd been amusing herself, twirling and swinging on the chains like a child, and he suppressed his grin.

Looking up, she saw her dom leaving. "Hey! David, where are you going? Hey!"

Simon paced forward. Slowly.

She saw him. Her eyes widened.

Perfect.

OH SWEET HEAVENS—Master Simon. As Rona stared at him, the laughter inside her fizzled out, and her heart began an annoyingly fast pace again.

His black gaze wandered over her, stroking her with heat. Her gown lay off to one side, but she hadn't felt particularly exposed—until now.

After setting down his big leather bag, Master Simon took off his coat and tossed it on a chair, leaving him in the white shirt and vest. His movements unhurried, he removed his cuff links. When they dropped onto the table with a metallic *clink*, Rona's breathing hitched.

He turned, rolling up his sleeves and exposing his muscular forearms.

Oh Crom. Wait, she started to say, but nothing came out of her frozen throat. She tried again. "Wait. You're not... I didn't... Where did David—the other guy—go?"

His dark eyes fixed on hers as he moved forward. "The other guy is a dom, but perhaps you got confused and thought him submissive." His level tone sent icy shivers down her spine. "I don't believe you'll make that mistake with me."

"I don't think—"

"Very good." He cut right through her sentence. The feel of his callous hand cupping her chin silenced her completely. "Thinking is my job, not yours. Your safe word is 'Houston.' Use it if something—mentally or physically—becomes too much for you."

She considered yelling it and took a breath.

His jaw tightened which dried up that notion instantly. "Don't toy with me, pet," he said softly.

She shook her head. *Not me. No, never.*

"I like that wide-eyed submissive look." His gaze ran over her. "In fact, I like seeing you in chains."

His words brought her attention to her restraints, and a quiver of fear joined the heat in her belly.

He cupped her cheek, his big hand disconcertingly gentle. "No, don't be frightened. We're just going to talk. First I want you to meet someone."

Master Simon glanced at a man standing off to one side and motioned him forward. Also in formal Victorian attire, the other man had coloring slightly darker than Simon's.

And as their attention turned to her, she felt like a mouse trapped in a feline festival. "Um. Hello?"

Master Simon's lips quirked. "Rona, this is Master Xavier, the owner of Dark Haven. Submissives here call him 'my Liege.'"

Her initial reaction—*you've got to be kidding*—died at the lack of expression in Xavier's calm, dark eyes.

"It's a pleasure to make your acquaintance, Rona," Master Xavier said, his voice quiet but easily heard over the myriad of noises.

"Pleased to meet you." *I love meeting people while standing around in my underwear.*

"Since we're immersed in the nineteenth century tonight, let me formally introduce you to Master Simon." A smile flickered on Xavier's lips. "He is well-known in the BDSM community, has an impeccable reputation as a dom. And I call him my friend."

The measured addition of the last part told her that Xavier didn't offer friendship lightly.

"Um." She glanced up at Simon. A crease appeared in his cheek as if he found her discomfiture amusing. Kicking him might be satisfying—if he didn't own a flogger. "Thank you, Xa—uh, my Liege. I appreciate the information."

Xavier nodded and walked away. No frivolous conversation for him.

And that left her with Master Simon. The sinking feeling in her stomach hadn't improved.

"Did you enjoy your tour, lass?" he asked politely.

Lass. Her grandfather from Glasgow had called her that, but coming from this utterly confident man, it made her feel funny— young and uncertain. And pretty. "Yes. It's an interesting place." He wanted to have a normal conversation with her standing here in chains?

"Have you tried BDSM before? At home, perhaps?"

On second thought, let's go back to normal. Her hands gripped the chains. "No. Never."

He stroked a finger across the nape of her neck, just under her bun. "Then I will give you your first lesson."

"But...why? Why me?" Every woman who walked by this man cast longing looks his way. *I'm not young. Or thin. Or gorgeous.*

"You, lass, have a self-image problem."

Well, that might be a little true, but she also had a mirror. It wasn't that she was ugly; it was that the competition was far too beautiful. And young. "Simon, I—"

His eyes narrowed, and her insides melted like ice cream on a sunny day. "I don't think I want you calling me Simon. Not in the club or when you're restrained...or in my bed."

The surge of excitement at the thought of being in his bed went all the way to her fingertips. And he'd done that deliberately, hadn't he? She sucked in a breath. *Keep your head in the game.* "What would you prefer?"

"You may call me 'Sir' or 'Master Simon.'" He brushed his fingers down her cheek. "I believe, for you, I'd permit a simple 'Master.'"

Master? No, that sounded way over-the-top. She shook her head.

"Oh, I think you will," he murmured. "Now let's talk about

what I see when I look at you."

Oh, let's not.

"First, you're not twenty...or even thirty." Almost absently, he removed one of the hairpins holding her bun in place, ignored her frown, and removed another. "But I like a woman with some life experience, one who isn't at the mercy of her emotions, and where a missed date or an argument doesn't constitute the ending of the world."

Remembering her son Eric's last meltdown when his new girlfriend had stood him up, Rona laughed.

"There, now. That's lovely," Simon said. Somehow the heat in his eyes slid right into her body. He ran a hand over her upper arm and squeezed gently. "I think muscles on a woman are beautiful, but I enjoy softness in my bed. And under me."

Everything he said sent more urgency curling through her body, and she lowered her gaze. "Well." Good grief, when had she become so inarticulate? She facilitated meetings full of prima donna doctors, for God's sake. She straightened her shoulders and gave him a level look. "I'm pleased that you—"

"Yes." He smiled at her. "Yes, that's exactly what I mean by experience. You don't crumple easily." Another pin slid out of her hair. "Rona, it is your choice, but I would be pleased to introduce you to whatever elements of BDSM interest you."

The man was smooth and dangerous, just like she'd thought. But oh so tempting. Her eyes dropped to his leather bag filled with...things, and a shiver ran through her. Let him do...something?

His lips curved. "Ah, now that was a yes." He pulled the last pin out, and her dark blonde hair fell down around her shoulders in a wavy mess. He tucked her pins into his vest pocket and raked his fingers through her hair. Each small tug sent tingles down her spine. "We will talk, and you can tell me what you like."

"Uh-huh." Tell him her fantasies? Not going to happen.

He stopped, and his finger under her chin lifted her gaze to his.

"Rona, first rule of a Dom-sub relationship: you share your thoughts, openly and honestly, hiding nothing."

"I don't know you."

"True. But you've heard me vouched for. You're attracted to me. Can you trust me enough to share what you found interesting in the club so far? Is that asking too much?"

She hadn't felt so cornered since the OR nurses had stormed her office about an instrument-throwing surgeon. "No. I can do that."

"Excellent. Considering your current position, obviously you find bondage and public display acceptable." He set his hand on her nape, his thumb curving around the side of her neck. His keen eyes focused on her face. "BDSM includes other pleasures. Like flogging."

As he'd done to that woman?

The laugh lines beside his mouth deepened. "Your pulse sped up. Excellent."

"Whipping."

She flinched. Earlier, she'd seen a dom use a long whip to create horrible red stripes on his victim. "No."

"Plain, bare-assed, bare-handed spankings."

She swallowed at the thought of being over a man's—Master Simon's—knees. Her fantasy list definitely needed revision. "Um, maybe."

"So everything except the whip." He nodded. "Then there's hot wax." He paused. "Piercing."

Needles? For fun? Hell no. She tried to pull away, and his hand gripped the back of her neck firmly. "Gently, lass. I'd say the wax is a maybe, but any piercing is a hard no. Is that right?"

Did he read everyone this easily or just her? She nodded.

His eyes crinkled, and then he brushed her mouth with his. His lips lingered, firm and velvety, and without any thought on her part, she tilted her head back for more.

"You are a sweet one," he murmured and took her face between his hands, holding her as his mouth urged hers open. He kissed her slowly. Deeply. Thoroughly.

With her wrists restrained, she was at his mercy, and the knowledge sent anticipation humming through her system.

He lifted his head to look at her for a long moment, then smiled and kissed her again until every drop of blood pooled in her lower half. Her body throbbed for more.

He moved a fraction of an inch back and caressed her cheek. "Where did I leave off? Ah, there are a variety of toys for fun like…a dildo. A vibrator. An anal plug."

Just the thought of someone using those on her made her squirm. "Maybe."

One side of his mouth curved up in a slight smile. "That was more than a maybe, lass. Have you ever used an anal plug?"

Her backside tensed, but with her hands chained over her head, she couldn't cover…anything. "No."

"I look forward to seeing your reaction. Did you happen to see the cupping earlier?"

Oh, she'd definitely seen that one. "Yes." Her voice came out husky.

He raised an eyebrow. "Interesting. And where else do you think a master might apply those cups?"

The dom had put them on his sub's back, but she'd imagined them on her nipples or even…on her clit. A wave of heat rolled into her face, as inevitable as the sun in summer.

He chuckled. "I'll enjoy that almost as much as you will."

"I didn't say yes." She hadn't, dammit.

"You didn't have to." He grasped the ribbon at the top of her chemise and pulled it open. Her nipples puckered.

"How about electrical play?"

All too aware of the warmth of his hand just above her breasts, she tried to concentrate on what he'd asked. "Electrical play?" She shook her head, then remembered the TENS unit a chiropractor had used on her sore back. Could those electrodes be placed elsewhere? Her vagina clenched, making her aware of how wet she'd become.

"Oh yes." The glint in his eyes made her stomach twist uneasily.

She swallowed. "Why so many questions for just one time?"

"There's always another time, pet. One more question." He studied her face as he ran his knuckles down the cleavage her chemise now exposed, and the closer his hand came to her breasts, the more her nipples tightened. "How about sex?"

Sex? Her breath caught. Sex with him? Every cell in her body jumped to life, waving pom-poms, and cheering. Her gaze dropped to his waist, to... She looked back up hastily. What was she thinking? "Uh no. I don't think so."

"Then, for tonight, I'll use only my hands." He didn't make it a question.

"Uh..." She nodded. Hands seemed safe enough. The thought of him taking her, being inside her... She wasn't ready for that intimacy. She might not be ready for this either.

"All right," he said easily. "We will begin." He strolled around her, and she could actually feel his gaze stroke over her thinly clad body. "You look lovely in Victorian undergarments, pet, but they're in my way." Without asking permission, he undid her corset, tiny hook by tiny hook, and tossed it onto a nearby table, leaving her in her chemise and drawers.

To her surprise, he ran his strong hands over her ribs, then massaged the painful ridges from the corset. She groaned from the relief. "Thank you."

His grin flashed, a moment of sunshine in the stern face. "I've heard they're uncomfortable." Reaching up, he unclipped her right wrist and lowered her arm. When he gathered up her chemise, she realized he planned to pull it over her head, baring her breasts.

She had one arm still chained, and her instinctive recoil got nowhere.

He raised his eyebrows.

With the other dom, David, she'd felt in control. Not with Master Simon. Lord, he didn't even speak, just looked at her, and her defiance oozed away. A sigh whispered out.

"Good girl," he said, his voice as soothing as a caress. After she slid her arm out of her chemise, he held out his hand, palm up.

She couldn't move for a second. Did she want him to chain her wrist back up? Her stomach shook in an internal earthquake. And then she set her hand in his.

Approval warmed his eyes. "This is what submission is, Rona," he said as he clipped her cuff to the overhead chain. "I can over-power you easily enough, but that's abuse. In domination, the only power I wield is what you freely give me."

After repeating the process with the other arm, he pulled the chemise over her head, leaving her bare from the waist up.

As the coolness brushed over her breasts, she looked around. Oh Lord, two doms and their subs had stopped to observe. A hot flush rose into her face. What was she doing here, letting herself be stripped?

"Look at me, pet."

Her gaze returned to him, and he held it until everything else faded except his dark eyes. He studied her for a long moment until her muscles stiffened with anticipation. Then he cupped a breast in each hand.

Oh Crom. Pleasure rushed through her like a tidal wave. Her nipples had been hard already and now tightened until they ached.

"You have lovely breasts, Rona." He paused and then frowned. "The correct response to a compliment is 'thank you, Sir.'"

"Thank you, Sir," she whispered. His gentle pinches on both nipples made her want to pull away with embarrassment and yet push forward for more. And she'd grown wet below, very wet.

As if he'd heard her thought, he put his boot between her bare feet and nudged her legs open. "Are your drawers traditional?"

When he ran a finger over her exposed skin just above the waistband, her stomach muscles quivered. "Traditional?"

"Crotchless?" He put his hand between her legs, right on her exposed pussy.

She gasped.

His grin flashed white in his tanned face. "I do love historical accuracy." He unhurriedly ran a finger through her wet folds, back and forth, never touching the one place that throbbed like mad. As her head spun, she started to draw her knees together and got another of those looks she'd begun to recognize.

"Don't move, pet, or I'll restrain your legs too."

She froze.

Her thighs quivered uncontrollably as his fingers explored her even more intimately, tracing over her clit, around her entrance. When he pushed a finger gently inside, she raised on tiptoes, stifling the moan in her throat.

"Very nice," he murmured, and she heard the approval in his deep voice through the swishing of her pulse in her ears. His finger eased farther into her, and his other hand touched her breast, tugging lightly on the nipple.

Oh Crom. Sheer, insane need swept over her like a landslide. When his thumb pressed on her clit, everything receded except the feeling of his hands on her. Her eyes closed as her insides gathered.

"No, not yet, sweetheart," he said. His touch lifted. "I want you a little on edge when I teach you about pain."

Her eyes flashed open. *Pain?*

The flogger he took from his bag didn't look like the same one he'd used before, but still—leather-covered handle, multiple blunt lengths of suede.

"You're going to whip me?" Her voice shook.

The dark eyes glinted with amusement. "Oh, I think so, yes." He brushed the flogger up her legs, her stomach, and teased the soft, dangling strands over her breasts until the peaks ached. The scent of leather filled the air as he lightly ran it up her arms and down her back, continuing until her skin grew so sensitive that each small caress sent a pulsing thrill through her.

The flogger brushed against her butt, and then the strands flipped across her bottom in the first blow.

She jumped. But it didn't hurt, didn't even sting. Instead the ends thudded against her skin like tiny hammers. More flicking touches moved down her legs and around to the front. As the lashes tapped slowly up her thighs, her heart started to pound. She pulled her legs together.

"Stay in position, or I will chain your ankles, pet." No anger, just a statement.

She moved her legs out. A little. Caught the expression in his eyes and opened them all the way, leaving her pussy dangerously vulnerable to those strands. A shudder went through her. Why didn't she use that safe word he'd given her?

But his intent gaze held her in place. And so did the way she felt—incredibly aroused—every nerve alive and singing with excitement.

He tucked the handle of the flogger into his waistband and moved closer. "You're being a good girl."

His hands cupped her breasts, his thumbs circling the nipples until a stream of electricity flowed straight to her clit. Her exposed clit. The open-legged position just begged for his touch. Her hips tilted forward, and she bit her lip, embarrassed. She wasn't like that, had never begged for anything. Ever. And yet... *Please touch me.*

He moved a hand to her pussy, sliding through her wetness. When his finger traced over her clit, she gasped at the sheer rush. But his finger eased away, gathered moisture, and then circled her clit. Around and around.

Pressure built inside her, and everything tightened, begging for just a little more. She moaned.

"Lovely," he murmured and stepped away. Before she could whimper a protest, the flogger struck her again, up and down her legs, front and back, then over her bottom, and a sting joined the thudding sensations. Not hurting, not really. Over her shoulders lightly and her hips, the blows circled her, and each time, the strands landed a little harder.

Still it didn't hurt, exactly, but she'd rather have his hands on her.

His eyes narrowed. "There goes that mind of yours, thinking away. You definitely need a tad more."

She caught her breath, hoping he'd touch her. Amazing how her inhibitions had disappeared.

Smiling slightly, he laid the flogger down next to his bag and pulled out a leather collar, fully as wide as his hand.

A collar? What kind of "more" was that?

He fitted it around her neck, adjusted her chin to rest in a small notch, and buckled it. Then he stood in front of her, caressing her cheek. Waiting.

He hadn't fastened it too snugly, and yet when she tried to move, she realized it raised her chin and kept her from looking either around or down. A flash of panic went through her and died at the steady look in his eyes.

"I won't leave you, sweetheart. If anything bothers you too much, use your safe word. Do you understand?"

She tried to nod and couldn't.

His eyes crinkled. "Say, 'Yes, sir.'"

"Yes, Sir."

"Good. Now you just stay put while I enjoy myself."

What did that mean? Her hands curled into balls as he knelt. With her chin held up by the collar, she couldn't see him. *The bastard.* Yet the arousal in her body edged up a notch as she waited for his touch. She had to wait; couldn't do anything else.

She heard a rustle, felt his hands on her pussy, and damn, it felt so good, his firm hands doing whatever he wanted. He buckled some sort of harness around her thighs and waist. Okay, that wasn't so bad, but then something pushed up inside her. Something cool. Hard. Not his fingers.

"What are you doing?" Her voice shook.

"Whatever I want, sweetheart." Liquid drizzled down her pussy, wet and cold, and she jumped. She felt a pinch over her clit, one that didn't release. Not painful but...disconcerting. A few clipping sounds and then tugs on the harness. "I'm just adjusting everything so it stays in place."

So what stays in place? She throbbed from the pressure of whatever was inside and from whatever sat over her clit. What was he doing?

When he stood, he had a microphone on his collar and a box— *a control box?*—clipped to his waistband.

Before she figured out what that combination meant, he ran his firm hands over her, stroking her skin, cupping her breasts, sending the warmth rising in her again. His lips settled on hers, and he took a long kiss. God, he could kiss. Her body relaxed...and heated.

He pulled back, smiled into her eyes, and then flipped a switch on the box.

Something made tapping sensations her clit and up inside her. Like tiny hammers. She jerked, her eyes wide. "What is that?"

"I'll show you in a bit. Your only job is to let me know if anything becomes uncomfortable." He put a finger on her chin and gave her an uncompromising look. "Otherwise I do not want to hear you speak. Am I clear, pet?"

She stiffened yet melted inside at his low, resonant voice and the commanding look in his eyes. "Yes, Sir."

As the tapping increased—somehow different from a vibrator, more inside than out—her clit tightened until it felt as if it would burst. Everything down there coiled, aching for more, and it wasn't enough. She smothered a moan. And she realized he'd stepped away to study her reactions.

He nodded. "Perfect." And then his flogger struck her thighs. The added sensation shocked through her and zoomed straight to her clit. Her legs tensed, and she rocked. He didn't stop. The leather strands hit lightly up her back, and each blow made the burning need in her pussy worse, so much worse.

She closed her eyes, swamped by the sensations.

He lashed her bottom, the backs of her thighs. "Rona."

With his words, the tingling on her clit increased in force and speed, and she moaned uncontrollably.

A second later the tapping abated. The flogger didn't. "Rona. Look at me."

Again, the vibrations intensified for a few seconds. Not nearly long enough. And the flogger never stopped, weaving a sensory spell around her. Up her legs, almost touching her pussy.

Oh God, just a little more. Her hands closed into fists, and her neck arched.

"Look. At. Me."

Again, the tapping strengthened, quickened, and the searing wave of arousal inside her and across her clit almost got her off, but then the vibrations slowed. She forced her eyes open.

His smile flashed in that chiseled face. "That's a girl."

Her back arched as the jump in sensations blew through her again. As they decreased, she stared at the mike clipped to his shirt. *Oh, Crom.* He could change the intensity of vibrations with his voice—with sound control.

The flogger struck her harder, each blow a flashing pain that stung and shunted more urgency through her until every nerve seemed swallowed by need. But she couldn't, couldn't get off. She whimpered. "Oh please…"

He chuckled, and just that tiny amount of sound shot through her like he'd pinched her clit.

Her hands clenched as she hovered on the pinnacle, with pain and pleasure so securely wound together, she just might die.

"All right, sweetie," he murmured.

Oh God, the feeling with his words. Sweat rolled down her back as she strained toward the climax she couldn't reach.

And then he said loudly, oh so loudly, "Let's hear you scream, pet." The vibrations turned exquisitely powerful inside and across her clit, and his flogger lashed across her breasts.

She exploded, wave after wave of blazing pleasure pouring

through every nerve in her body, shaking her like a rag doll. Her legs simply collapsed.

"Very nice," he said, and the sound kicked off more vibrations. As the intense spasms shocked through her, she couldn't move, couldn't do anything except feel each rippling wave. When they finally stopped, she hung limply from the chains, her mind hazed. Satisfied. Stunned.

She barely registered his removing everything, undoing the harness on her thighs, then the collar. Too heavy to stay upright, her head rested against her chained arm.

"Hang on another minute, lass." He unchained her wrists and caught her around the waist when she'd have folded right onto the floor. A second later her brain went into a roller-coaster swirl. She blinked in astonishment—*he's carrying me?*—and stared up at his corded neck and strong jaw. Rock-hard arms held her against his solid chest, and the scent of his subtly musky cologne surrounded her. The disconcerting sense of fragility blended with the wonderful feeling of being cherished.

Chapter Three

NOW WASN'T SHE the nicest armful he'd had in a long time? The way her body fit against his made Simon wonder if their personalities would match equally well. Logical or not, everything inside him said yes.

He took a seat in a nearby leather chair and settled her comfortably on his lap. Her soft ass pressed against his painfully rigid cock, and she obviously felt it. "What about you?" she murmured. "Can I—"

"No, sweetheart." He kissed the top of her head, warmth seeping into him both from her body and from the knowledge that she wanted to give back as well as to receive. "This evening was for your pleasure."

And for his, in a way. He'd enjoyed introducing her to BDSM more than anything he'd done in a long time. He smiled, remembering how the wariness in her eyes had warred with the arousal of her body. When she had set her hand in his, the trust she'd given him had squeezed his heart.

He rubbed his chin on her silky hair, pleased with her light fragrance of vanilla and citrus that created the feeling of a garden within the wilderness of the club. Her cheek rested against his chest, and she gripped the front placket of his old-fashioned shirt as if she feared he'd leave her. Not a chance.

But he shouldn't let her get too comfortable. This woman

needed to be kept off balance, at least for now. So he contracted his grip and ran his free hand over her bare breasts, smiling when she startled.

"Don't move, pet," he cautioned her.

Sweetly submissive, she stilled, although her breathing increased.

He pleased himself with the feel of her round breasts. Despite her recent orgasm, her satiny nipples responded quickly, forming dark pink peaks. When he pinched one, she quivered and looked up at him.

Her turquoise-colored eyes were very vulnerable in the aftermath of the scene and roused all his protective instincts. Odd. He hadn't felt this intensely about anyone since the birth of his son. He kissed her lightly, reassuringly, and felt her muscles relax.

"Did you like your first experience with BDSM?" he asked. He knew one answer, considering how hard she'd come, but a woman's fears and worries couldn't be plumbed in just one evening.

"Well. I… Yes, I did."

No coy answers from this sub. Damn, she pleased him.

He stroked her cheek, holding her gaze. "What part did you like the most?"

She stiffened, obviously unused to intimate questions. She'd have to learn better. Not only did he require it as a dom, but also as a lover. And he wanted to know her all the way down to her soul. He tightened his grip and moved his hand back to her breasts, increasing their physical intimacy to match the emotional. "Answer me."

Her body softened at his firm order. *Submissive.* But still silent.

"All right, I'll help. Did you like the flogging?" He ran his hand under her round ass to where he'd struck the hardest, and squeezed her undoubtedly sore flesh.

She jumped.

"Or the electrical play?" He touched her still-wet pussy, enjoying the drifting scent of her arousal.

Her body stiffened, and she tried to sit up, but his arm around her shoulders kept her in place. She was going nowhere. He ran his fingers up and down her swollen labia and grazed the vulnerable little clit.

She inhaled sharply.

Was she this responsive with everyone, or did her body also recognize the connection between them? "Do I need to show you the choices again?"

Two people walking past overheard and laughed.

Her cheeks flushed a lovely pink. She cleared her throat. "No. The electrical stuff. Only, if I'd known you wanted to do that, I—"

"You'd never have allowed an electrode anywhere near this pretty pussy?"

"Crom no."

Crom. He'd heard that odd word used as a soft curse one time before. Where? Then he smiled slowly as he remembered. "The riot after the football game."

"Excuse me?"

"Last year, you helped my son when he got hurt in the riot." While Simon had fought the surging crowd from trampling Danny, Rona had braced his son's broken arm and checked him for other injuries. Her low, soft voice had been compassionate, and her matter-of-fact tone, reassuring. She'd directed her two teenage boys to help Danny stand, so Simon could get him out of the mess. Then, trailed by her sons, she'd moved on to assist others. Danny still called her his football angel.

"Oh." She frowned at him. "I don't remember you."

"You concentrated on my son." He rubbed his chin against her wavy hair. A ball cap had hidden it that night, and she'd worn jeans and a high school letter jacket. No wonder he hadn't recognized her. "What is a Crom, anyway?"

When she gave a husky laugh, he grinned. He'd been right, her voice had indeed deepened after she'd come. "It's the god of Conan the Barbarian. My superhero-worshipping sons and I decided Crom wouldn't mind if we took his name in vain."

"Ah." Both practical and quirky. "Well, my son and I thank you for your help that night." He kissed her gently for thanks, then continued, teasing her mouth, savoring the softness, the willingness to enjoy, and the delightful skill with which she ran her tongue over his lips, alternating with gentle nibbles.

When he slid one finger over her clit, she gave the softest of moans. Perhaps they weren't finished after all, and now that he knew more about her, he was damned if he wanted to stop.

He gently pinched her clit between his fingers. When she gasped, he took possession of her mouth, hard and deep, even as he slipped a finger into her. After pulling his hand back, he thrust harder into her and felt the surging arousal of her body.

After ending the kiss, he smiled down at her. Her eyes had glazed with passion; her lips were red and wet. The hand she'd wrapped behind his neck resisted his movement away even as her pussy contracted around his finger. Passionate and responsive. Intelligent, brave, and submissive. Her appeal grabbed him by the guts and pulled. He took a slow, steady breath. "Let me clean up the scene area, and we'll find somewhere else to play." The Victorian Room would serve nicely, considering the theme tonight, and she'd look lovely bound to the four-poster.

Her eyes widened and then narrowed. He could almost hear her brain switch back on.

RONA PUSHED HERSELF to a sitting position, dismayed at her behavior. She'd wanted to explore, but jumping right in like this... What had she been thinking? She didn't really know this man, and he'd kept touching her as if she belonged to him. Crom, his finger still filled her, eroding her resistance. She grasped his thickly corded wrist and tried to push his hand away.

His arm didn't budge an inch. In fact, he deliberately pressed in farther until his palm brushed against her throbbing clit.

A spasm of delight sent heat soaring through her like she'd entered a sauna. She sucked in a lungful of air, wanting nothing so much as to say, *More.* "Stop, please."

His head tilted. His dark eyes had never left hers. He slid his finger from her, ever so slowly, his gaze studying her.

She felt the warmth of an embarrassed flush. He knew exactly how turned on he'd made her, dammit.

His lips quirked, but the arm around her loosened. He wasn't going to push her.

She breathed a sigh of relief until he lifted his hand and licked the finger that glistened with her wetness, sampling it like a fine vintage.

"You taste as hot and sweet as I thought you would." His eyes left her no doubt that he imagined his mouth replacing his hand.

Her vagina clenched, feeling only emptiness where he'd been. Everything in her burned for his touch. *Take me. No.* Her thoughts jiggled in her head like a heart in atrial fibrillation until she finally remembered why she needed to leave. The second item on her "I'm free to change" goals: for at least one year, she could only have sex with a man once before moving on to a new guy. She'd decided to take no chance of getting caught or stuck in a rut.

Not even with someone like this. *Especially with someone like this.* She firmed her lips and pushed off his lap and onto her feet.

He frowned but rose in instinctive courtesy. Unfortunately, that left her looking up at him. His shoulders broad and muscular. He could overpower her easily, and damn her for wanting him to. Damn him for being so devastating.

"I really must go," she said firmly, despite the flutters in her stomach. "Thank you for the sample of BDSM, Master Simon. I…learned a lot."

"You view this as a lesson only?" His eyes narrowed. "Was I mistaken in the impression that you enjoyed yourself?"

Considering how she'd screamed, he knew full well she'd gotten off. And yet his words still made her feel guilty, as if she was being rude. "I did enjoy myself. But…"

"Continue."

Authoritative jerk, she thought, and yet every time his voice took on that commanding tone, she wanted to roll over and go belly up like her neighbor's wimpy dachshund. "I won't do anything with anyone more than once."

"So, good or bad, each man gets only one shot?"

"That's right. That's my rule." Posted on the bulletin board at home, no less.

"I see." His hand curved around the nape of her neck as if she were a kitten being dragged by its mother. "Rona, I would like to see you again. If you prefer to avoid…intimate…surroundings, I'll take you to dinner."

"No. But thank you." She gave him a firm nod and held out her hand, pretending she still had on clothing. "I enjoyed meeting you."

His mouth thinned into a hard line…but it hadn't been hard at all when he kissed her. His fingers on her neck tightened, and then he released her.

"It was nice meeting you too, lass." He took her hand, turned it over, and grazed his lips over her palm, sending a rush straight to her pussy. Damn, he was potent. His gaze brushed over her blatantly peaked nipples, and a corner of his mouth tipped up. "We'll talk soon about this rule of yours."

She could see he expected her to argue over that statement, but she'd lived long enough to know the utility of a quick retreat. Especially since her body had started a raging argument with her head.

When she pulled her hand away, he let her go. He ran a finger down her cheek, the look in his eyes so intense, it felt as if he'd touched her soul. And yet gentle. Caring.

More shaken by that look even than her arousal, she slung her hoop over her shoulder and grabbed her clothing and shoes. Clutching everything to her bare chest, she marched through the place, up the stairs, and to the changing rooms near the front. Once there, she leaned her back against the cool metal of a locker and sighed.

Why did he have to be so...so overwhelming? Every time he gave her one of those commanding looks, she wanted to fall at his knees and say, *Take me. Please.* Was she that much of a weak-willed female?

Oh yes. When it came to him, definitely yes.

And that last look he'd given her... She'd better stick with easier men to date or the first item on her list—*not get involved with anyone for at least five years*—wouldn't last a month.

Chapter Four

THE DRENCHING MORNING rain had given way to clear skies, and now the late-afternoon sun warmed Rona's shoulders. She strolled down the center of the blocked-off avenue, dodging the others also enjoying this pre-Christmas street fair. The raunchy lyrics of Hollywood Undead blasted out from a boom box down the street. Sex toys, fet-wear, bondage equipment—this was the place to shop for a loved one whose tastes edged into kinky. Or if you wanted to indulge in buying for yourself.

She glanced at a man leading another by a leash and grinned. Who would have thought she'd find such things tempting? Her trip to Dark Haven two weeks ago had opened her eyes in many ways.

And complicated her life. She frowned. Hoping to get that overbearing, *commanding*, overmuscled, *gorgeous*, man, *dom*, out of her thoughts, she'd gone on a flurry of dates. And each evening had been as exciting as giving a patient a bed bath.

Had just one taste of BDSM spoiled her for normal guys? The memory of how Master Simon's dark eyes had studied her as he cuffed her wrists sent a blast of heat through her like she'd sniffed a vial of pheromones.

Of course, the sights and sounds around her didn't help. She dodged an extremely tall man in a cat suit and cat mask, then a cluster of men in chain harnesses and jeans. Shrugging her canvas shopping bag to a comfortable position on her shoulder, she checked out the booths displaying garter belts, vinyl and latex clothing, and costumes. She wanted something exotic so she could blend in next time she went to Dark Haven. Maybe a sexy bustier?

She paused by a stall that sold sex toys. So many times she'd considered getting a vibrator, but it had seemed a kind of betrayal of Mark, no matter how flat their love life had grown. But now…

Several women clustered around the stall, decreasing her feeling of being conspicuous. *Look, Rona's going to buy a vibrator!* Edging to the front, she studied the offerings. *Where to start?* Dildos ranged from tiny—*why would anyone use something the size of a finger?*—to a terrifying one that resembled a foot-long mushroom and made her vagina cringe, if such a thing were possible.

Then she noticed the vibrator section. Oh yes. Right off her fantasy list—which had grown remarkably after her club visit. Tiny balls to go inside. *Nah.* Some the size and shape of a real cock. Her finger tapped her lips. Too bland. She spotted one that could be used in both orifices. Her butt constricted at the thought, but… *Hmm…* Next to it lay a combination dildo-and-clit vibrator, and her bottom actually wiggled at the idea. She started to reach for it…

A hand pressed against her lower back, and a deep, smooth voice murmured in her ear, "I'm going to get the wrong impression of you if we keep meeting in these types of venues."

She caught the scent of sensuously rich cologne before she jerked around and stared up into dark eyes that glinted with amusement. "Ma—Simon."

"Ah. I haven't been forgotten completely."

When he stroked a finger down her cheek, her insides quivered as if the fabled San Francisco quake had started. Nice trick, that. She doubted if even the fancy vibrators in the booth could achieve such an effect. "What are you doing here?"

"Some friends are giving a demonstration of suspension bondage." He glanced at his watch. "I have fifteen minutes free. May I join you?"

Oh yes. Then her brain kicked in. *Oh no.*

He shook his head. "So divided." Lifting a finger, he attracted the attention of the booth owner, picked up the combination vibrator, and handed her some money.

Rona eyed the device. A guy wouldn't use something like that, would he? No. So he'd bought it for a girlfriend or... "Are you married?"

When he cocked an eyebrow at her blunt question, she sighed. At work, she'd been described as confident and articulate, yet in his presence, she tripped over her tongue like a verbal spastic.

"No, I'm not married, lass. Or in any relationship whatsoever."

Wasn't he going to ask her that question in return? Her mouth turned down. Didn't he want to know?

Smiling, he lifted her hand and tapped the fading mark on her ring finger where her wedding band had been. "I don't need to ask, lass. And you're too honest to scene with me if you were involved."

"Both telepathy and X-ray vision, huh?"

He chuckled. "I've been a dom for quite a while. Eventually you learn to use your eyes."

As the seller counted out his change, a shriek split through the noise of the crowd. Rona turned.

Near the center of the street, two brawling, red-faced men had knocked an older lady to her knees. As "fuck yous" filled the air, they tried to tear each other apart, heedless of their victim.

Worse than Saturday night in the ER. Growling in disgust, Rona dodged around the men to get to the woman. Slinging an arm around the frail waist, Rona pulled her up and out of the battle zone. Looking over her shoulder to make sure she'd gone far enough, Rona gaped.

Standing between the two men, Simon had stopped the fight. For a second. Then one swore and lunged around Simon to attack the other.

Shaking his head, Simon shoved up his sleeves, stepped forward, and...

Rona blinked. His fists had moved too fast to follow, but now one man lay moaning on the ground, arms wrapped around his stomach. Simon had the other on his knees, his hand clamped in the man's hair. From the way the jerk's arm dangled, his shoulder was dislocated.

With a tiny quiver, Rona recognized the stern set to Simon's jaw as he talked to the brawler in a low voice. When he stepped back, the brawler scrambled to his feet and fled through the gathered crowd.

Simon dragged the other one to a sitting position. After saying a few words, he hauled the guy to his feet and shoved him on his way. Apparently oblivious to the scattered applause from the crowd, Simon rolled down his sleeves and retrieved his purchase.

When he joined Rona, his intent gaze scrutinized her, top to bottom, before he turned to the old woman. "Are you all right, ma'am?"

"I am now." The lady smiled at him. "You did a fine job there. Thank you."

"My pleasure."

"Well, I need to move along. I still have to get a present for Henry." The woman brushed the dirt from her lavender sweats and frowned at the rip in one knee. "Our fortieth anniversary is tomorrow, and we buy each other a treat every year." She nodded at Simon, patted Rona's shoulder in thanks, and walked toward the toy booth.

Rona stared. The treat for Henry was a sex toy? After forty years of marriage? *Damn.*

Simon huffed a laugh, then wrapped an arm around Rona's waist. "Come, lass."

"Where'd you learn to fight like that?"

He steered her down the street. "Military, then the martial-arts circuit for a time. I quit when my son arrived." He lifted his left hand, tried to curl the fingers, and smiled ruefully. "I fear I hit a few too many solid objects before then."

Frowning, Rona took his hand. White scars from old surgeries traced over his skin; the bones underneath felt rough and uneven. "You must have broken every…" She looked up guiltily, let go, and put her hands behind her back. *Bad Rona.* Hadn't she already learned that grabbing a dom was a no-no? "Sorry."

His flashing smile lightened his face. "True, a submissive doesn't touch without permission." When he grasped her hand and ran his thumb over her knuckles, the suggestive caress sent a tingle through her. "But I enjoy having your hands on me too much to object. For now."

"For now?"

He threaded his fingers into her hair and tugged her head back, forcing her to look up at him. "I think, eventually, I will enjoy reprimanding you just as much. Your ass turns such a pretty pink."

Before she could speak, he gave her a hard kiss and released her.

She stared at him, the sheer heat his words had engendered burning away any sarcastic response.

Smiling, he took her hand and started walking again. "The stage is down this way."

"Simon. We're not dating."

"We will." He ran his thumb over her lower lip, and the carnal look in his eyes dried up all the saliva in her mouth.

She looked away, concentrating on her walking. *I'm not attracted. Really.* And that's like claiming that Lois Lane never really wanted Superman. Nonetheless, *remember rules one and two from the goals list.* "Simon. I appreciate the trouble you've taken, but I'm not interested in…in anything more."

She winced at the thoughtful look in his eyes. Despite the noisy crowd and the brightly colored booths, all his attention was now focused on her, nowhere else, with an unsettling concentration.

"You're attracted to me," he said so confidently that she glanced down to see if she wore a sign saying I WANT YOU. "And you're not involved a relationship. So…?"

Obstinate, wasn't he? "I was married for twenty years. The last few years, we just tolerated each other until our children left the nest, and when they did, we got a divorce. I promised myself I'd never get trapped like that again."

He raised an eyebrow.

"Being married…" It had been like wading through a dark swamp, unable to find a way out. "I have a new life. I'm free to explore and experience everything I missed. That includes a variety of men."

"Ah."

OBSTINATE, WASN'T SHE? Simon shook his head.

She lifted her stubborn chin and lengthened her stride, as if she could shake him so easily. She couldn't. Not after the way his body and heart had leaped when he'd seen her in the crowd. He stepped around a bare-chested gay couple dancing to Combichrist and rejoined her.

Unfortunately, he understood how escaping a cage might make a woman wary about being caught again. It would take some clever bread crumbs to lure her closer.

And he wanted her closer. Even if he disregarded that unexpected connection from before, she attracted him. She'd helped his son at the riot and rescued the old woman with no hysterics or screaming, just compassion and practicality. And she could have claimed involvement with someone but hadn't. She might not share her emotions freely, but what she shared would be honest. And that was as unusual as it was appealing.

He wanted her in his life, wanted to see if they matched as well as he believed.

No, he wouldn't let her run away, not if the need to explore proved to be her only objection. He smiled down at her, thinking of how she'd look cuffed to his bed while they…explored. But deeply held opinions rarely changed with logical arguments. So for now, his plan must be to keep her near, and he just happened to have the perfect way to do that.

As they neared the stage, he stopped. "Rona, this coming Saturday, I'm holding my annual Christmas party for those in the lifestyle." He touched her cheek and caught a trace of her citrus and vanilla scent—tangy and sweet, well suited to her. "I'd be pleased if you'd come. You will meet plenty of unattached doms."

"Really? Even though I said no to…seeing you?"

"Even though." He wanted to see what they had in common—and what they'd fight about. He already knew she'd be an interesting opponent, forthright and clever. He might deliberately lose an argument just to hear her husky laugh. Then again, considering her obvious intelligence, she'd probably win all by herself. He pulled an invitation from his wallet. "Since you're new, I'll make sure you don't get in over your head."

"Well. Thank you. I'll think about it." From the flare of excitement in her eyes, he knew she was hooked. He'd have time to convince her to give them both a chance at happiness. And those soft curves would feel wonderful under him.

Smiling at that thought, he handed her the bag containing the rabbit vibrator he'd bought. "I got this for you, lass."

"You what?"

"I would have enjoyed showing you how it works, but since you prefer otherwise, you may simply think of me when you use it. Tonight." Before she could recover from the shock, he kissed her lightly on her soft, soft lips and walked away.

THE LUNCH CROWD in the hospital cafeteria had thinned quite a bit by the time Rona managed to cut free of her phone and e-mails. The scattered tables held a spattering of nurses in scrubs, med students, two surgeons between cases, and a few visitors. She set her tray on the small table and sat down across from her friend. "I hate hump day."

Brenda laughed and dipped a french fry in ketchup. "Me too.

Speaking of humping, did you know that Charles Madigan got a divorce?"

"Really?" Rona dumped a sparing amount of ranch dressing on her healthy salad. Dieting was tiresome, but the anticipation of baring…everything…this weekend proved more than sufficient incentive.

"Makes good money, our age, single, gorgeous. Why aren't you looking interested?"

"He's all right, but I want…more."

Brenda frowned. "*More* like in that bar you went to?"

Rona laughed at the disapproving tone. "Uh-huh."

"And how the hell do you figure on finding…more? You got a plan mapped out, Ms. Obsessive-Compulsive."

"Thanks a lot. You know, if you don't write down what you want, you'll never know if you get there." Rona nudged aside the insipid-looking excuse for a tomato, then speared some romaine leaves. "Actually, a man invited me to a party." She snickered. "A *more* party."

"Oh…my." The brunette pointed with a french fry. "Did you meet him at that club?"

"Yes." The memory of Simon's implacable voice threatening to chain her legs apart sent heat through her body in a mighty wave. Knowing she'd turned red, Rona lowered her head and poked at her salad. "And again at a street fair." *Where he bought me a vibrator. And told me to think of him while using it…* Oh, she certainly had. The jerk had known she would.

"Twice? And now a party? Ooooh, this sounds good."

"No." When eagerness to see him roused, Rona stomped it flat. "I'm not going for him. I want to meet other guys. Getting involved isn't in my plans."

"So enjoy him without getting involved. Like Max does." Brenda jerked her chin toward the surgeon. He was notorious for his having affairs with several women simultaneously, although he'd discovered the dangers of dating two OR nurses at once.

Rona studied him with rising hope. That might just work. "Sex with Simon one night, then with someone else a day or so later, and so on. No way could anything get serious."

"That's the spirit."

Boy, it sounded a bit—*a lot*—slutty, but making up for lost years wasn't for sissies. And tonight she'd revise the rule list: *No sexy seconds unless dating additional men.*

Chapter Five

ON SATURDAY EVENING, Rona walked through the open front door of Simon's three-story, stone-and-stucco house. A myriad of guests stood in small groups under a huge sparkling chandelier, and laughter and conversation filled the foyer. The party had definitely started.

"Merry Christmas!" A young woman in an elf costume with bright green fishnet stockings hurried across the gleaming dark wood floor.

At the high-pitched greeting, people glanced toward Rona. A second later a man disengaged from a small group and strode across the room. Master Simon.

Rona pulled in a breath as her nerves went on alert as if someone had called a code blue for a heart attack.

Arriving first, the elf beamed at Rona. "Come on. I'll take you around."

"Mandy, I'll show her to the dressing room," Master Simon said as he stopped behind the elf. He squeezed the young woman's shoulder. "Thank you, pet."

The elf gazed up at him in adoration, then scurried away, the white pom-pom on her red hat bouncing with each step.

Simon watched her for a second, and he murmured, "So much energy." Then his black gaze turned toward Rona like a dark laser beam, the type that would cut a villain right in half.

Her heart gave a violent *thud*. The man had dressed simply, in black slacks and a white shirt that set off his dark tan, yet when a smile lightened his stern face, her blood fizzed in her veins like a shaken Coke.

"Rona. I'm pleased you came." He held out his hand, waiting patiently until she gave him hers. His fingers closed, encasing her in warmth.

"Thank you for the invitation," she said, falling back on proprieties. She caught sight of his guests and frowned. Although the dominants remained fully clothed in jeans or suits or leathers, all the submissives were in elf costumes. One wore only a Santa hat and red nipple clamps. *Oh Crom.* Rona's stomach sank as she glanced down at her slinky black dress.

Growing up, she couldn't afford the trendy clothing her friends wore, and had hated never fitting in. Shallow or not, her feelings hadn't changed. She stepped back. "I don't think that I—"

He chuckled. "Relax, pet. I took the liberty of selecting an outfit for you."

An elf pranced by wearing only red high heels, a red thong, and a hat. Rona winced. *Do I even want to know what he got me?*

Ignoring her hesitation, he set a hand on her low back and steered her across the foyer to a powder room. "I left your costume on the counter in one of my company bags—look for a Demakis International Security logo."

"Well." All arranged. He'd obviously put some thought into making her comfortable. "Thank you."

"I think a more enthusiastic expression of gratitude is in order." With one finger, he tilted up her chin. Before she could protest, firm lips explored hers, teasing for a response. When she sighed and leaned toward him, he yanked her against his solid body and took the kiss from sweet to devastatingly possessive.

Crom. Her memories hadn't come close to how he really kissed or how easily he could control her. Heat pooled in her belly like molten lava.

When he pulled back and steadied her on her feet, she was breathing like an asthmatic having an acute attack.

"Now that was a very nice thank-you," he murmured. "Go change, lass. Then meet me in the living room. I'll explain the rules and introduce you around."

As he pushed her gently into the powder room, she frowned. *Rules?*

A

IN THE LIVING room, Simon did the rounds, greeting his guests, making introductions. Along with the local BDSMers, quite a few friends had arrived from out of town. Busy or not, he kept an eye on the arched doorway, his anticipation rising. He spotted Rona the minute she walked into the room.

She paused in the doorway. Her hands rubbed the white fur downward in a nervous gesture, although her face appeared serene and self-confident. To come to a party by herself, to try something so new... Brave lass.

And she looked beautiful. A fuzzy red Santa cap with a white puff ball at the end sat on her wavy blonde hair. The long-sleeved, red velvet coat trimmed with white fur reached only to the top of her creamy white thighs. Right where he wanted his hand. If she bent over, everyone would have an enticing glimpse of the ribbon-tied, peppermint-striped bra and thong set he'd bought.

Wanting her to feel comfortable, he'd chosen relatively conservative clothing. Of course, being a dom, he'd selected for his own pleasure also.

The wide sleeves would accommodate wrist cuffs, and only a securely fastened leather belt held the buttonless coat closed. Poor sub. Belt and ribbons could and would be removed over the course of the evening. He hardened at the thought of revealing those sweet curves.

When she spotted him, her eyes lit up in a way that made his chest compress. Her head might tell her not to get involved, but apparently her emotions matched his. He'd do his best to see that her emotions won.

He crooked a finger, then grinned as her passage across the room netted interested glances from the dominants.

One stepped away from her friends. Tara gave Rona a long look. "Oh, that's nice. Tell me she likes girls and not boys."

"No," Simon told the tall domme, not looking away from his sub. "She's straight."

Tara's eyebrows went up. "Well, well. I haven't seen that look in your eyes in a long time...if ever." She slapped his arm in approval before returning to her group.

Rona stopped in front of Simon.

"You look lovely," he said and enjoyed how her cheeks turned pink.

"Thank you. And thank you for...for giving me enough costume."

"You are very welcome." He tugged her silky hair lightly. "Do bear in mind that submissives usually wind up wearing less clothing by the end of a party."

The wary look she gave him included a fair amount of excitement. "I'm not sure I understand."

"These are the rules: as is normal for a submissive at a party, you will serve the doms food and drinks. Since you're not owned, a dom may touch any part of you that isn't covered." He grinned when her arms wrapped protectively around the coat. "Touch only, pet. Scenes and intimate play must be negotiated. The safe word in my house is 'red.' Some doms and subs have their own safe words, but if someone shouts 'red' in here, everyone shows up to enforce it."

"That's both scary and reassuring," she said.

Smart girl. Despite all the precautions, BDSM still hovered on the dangerous side. "Before playing, you will inform the dom of your inexperience. But as an additional precaution, I had this made for you." He pulled the gold necklace from his pocket and put it around her neck. It settled just below her throat.

She picked up the lettered part and tucked her chin down to read it. *Elf-in-training.* Her laugh was husky and open.

Would she laugh during sex? He'd given her intense; how about playful? He shoved the question aside. "Now, who would you like to meet?"

RONA CHATTED WITH an older dom named Michael in the great room. During the past hour, she'd wandered around, just observing the interesting scenes going on. Master Simon had scattered BDSM equipment over the entire first floor for the party. Tables and spanking benches with various forms of restraints were in the living and dining rooms, a massive St. Andrew's cross stood in the center of his great room. The large granite-countered kitchen held a stockade, and chains dangled from the exposed beams. All set up to entice people to play.

So, dammit, why couldn't she find a dom who was half the man Master Simon was? Whenever he entered the room, she could feel his presence—a shimmering aura of power. His gaze would sweep the room and settle on her. He'd look her over so thoroughly, she'd feel the heat rise in her cheeks. And then he'd turn away.

Leaving her alone, as he'd promised.

That was what she wanted, right? She really did need to have a few more men on her string before indulging in hot, roaring sex with him. Just the thought made her mouth dry. *Bad sign, Rona.*

Time to jump into the party spirit and stop stalling. She smiled at the man beside her. Maybe she'd start with him.

"Doms." Master Simon's voice filled the room, making her breath hitch. "If you are not occupied, I need assistance judging the first contest. Any uncollared elves who are not busy, please line up here."

A contest? Great. Unless he planned something intellectual, she'd surely lose. She hesitated.

A hand closed on her arm, and she looked up at the gray-haired dom beside her.

Michael frowned at her. "Simon might have said 'please,' but it wasn't a request, sub; it was an order." He pulled her across the room to Master Simon.

"She wanted to think it over before obeying," Michael said and let her go.

"Really." Master Simon's eyes darkened with displeasure.

Oh Crom. "I don't like contests. I lose," she said hurriedly. Why did his disapproval make her chest tighten and her stomach sink? She looked down.

"I see." He lifted her chin, forcing her to meet his gaze. "Unfortunately, your opinion doesn't count, does it."

He hadn't really asked a question, but she answered anyway. "No."

His fingers flexed on her chin just enough to remind her of her manners.

"No, Sir. I'm sorry, Sir."

"Much better." He released her. "Join the others."

As she took her place at the end of the line, he said, "This submissive contest is for general friendliness and service." He grasped the first sub by her nape and asked the crowd, "If this pretty elf either gave you her name or served you in any way, please raise your hand."

Seven hands lifted, mostly dommes'.

Rona bit her lip as uneasiness twisted her insides. Concentrated on getting her bearings, she'd spoken casually with a few doms but hadn't introduced herself.

Soon she realized the other elves had stayed very busy, serving drinks and food, giving back rubs, foot rubs, or playing with a dom as requested. Very few hadn't done much; unfortunately, she was one of them.

Master Simon gripped the back of her neck firmly, pulling her a step closer to him. She shivered as his hard chest brushed against her shoulder and his warm, rich scent surrounded her. He asked the crowd, "And this sub?"

Only Michael lifted his hand.

"Ah. Well, she is just in training, after all. Please help her out and put her to work, gentlemen." His hand dropped away. "All elves who earned more than five raised hands, you've done well. You're dismissed. The rest of you slackers, remove one article of clothing and leave it on the table there."

When three-quarters of the subs dispersed, Rona sighed in relief. At least she wasn't the only slacker. *Remove something.* Well, she hated wearing hats anyway. Her hand had just touched the fuzzy cap when Master Simon added casually, "I should mention that if I find an elf without an elf cap, I will toss her out on the street...naked."

Rona snatched her hand away and heard him chuckle. Crom, she didn't have much to choose from. Maybe she could remove her bra in the powder room?

"You have ten seconds, and then we'll all help."

Maybe she didn't like Master Simon after all.

"Ten. Nine—"

Jaw clenched, Rona unbuckled and pulled her belt off.

"One."

She tossed the belt on the table. Lacking buttons, her Santa coat fell open, displaying her very skimpy bra and thong. She'd have to hold it shut all night. *That jerk.*

Looking around, she saw one elf must have waited too long. Three doms had surrounded her and were stripping her of clothing. Rona bit her lip, trying to decide if she'd find that exciting or frightening. She rubbed her chilled hands on her coat.

"Rona," Master Simon said.

"Sir?"

"Please take a filled tray from the kitchen and serve drinks until it's empty."

Cool. Something active to do. "Yes, Sir. Thank you, Sir."

He grinned.

In the kitchen, when she picked up the tray, she understood his amusement. Holding the tray required both hands, and now she couldn't hold her coat shut. "You bastard," she muttered.

"Excuse me?"

She whirled so suddenly that the drinks sloshed.

"Did I mention the rule about speaking without permission?" His eyes glinted with laughter.

"Yes, Sir."

He smiled slowly. "You're penalized one ribbon." Reaching over her tray of drinks, he tugged on the ribbon serving as the left strap for her bra. The bow came undone, and he pulled the ribbon out of the grommets.

Held up on only one side, her bra sagged, exposing her left breast.

Still holding the tray, she looked up at him.

"I like that helpless look," he murmured and ran his fingers down her neck to her bared breast.

Her attempt at retreat only backed her into the kitchen island. Trapped between it and him, she stared over his shoulder as he stroked her breast, circling the peak with one finger. She could feel her nipple pebbling under his confident touch. How it ached.

A gentle pinch made her jump; the glasses chimed on the tray. Her eyes jerked up, and he held her gaze as his fingers teased her nipple. When he squeezed the tip, a hot sizzle shot straight to her groin. Her fingers locked on the tray as he increased the pressure— as her excitement skyrocketed.

His eyes crinkled. "We need to get you into a scene before you explode," he said softly. He brushed his lips over hers and stepped back. "Go serve, lass. If you find someone you'd like to top you, I'll release you from your duty."

As she walked through the rooms, everyone greeted her politely. Some took a glass; some ignored the drinks and made themselves free with her body, running their hands over any exposed skin. The air around her grew increasingly warm.

In the living room, she spotted Michael talking to two tough-looking doms in black leathers. A redheaded sub knelt on the floor between their chairs.

"Rona." Michael waved her closer. "This is Logan"—he nodded toward the dom with steel blue eyes and dark brown hair—"his sub, Rebecca, and his brother, Jake."

Jake looked as hard and lean as his brother but had a nasty scar across his tanned forehead that his thick hair couldn't hide. He considered her for a long moment, then cocked a brow. "That's a nice elf costume, blondie."

Uncertain as to how she should address them, she said, "I'm pleased to meet you, Sirs."

"Your arrival is timely." Michael grinned. "We're arguing about where a woman's legs are the most sensitive. I think it's behind the knee. Jake says just below the ass."

Rona frowned. Did he expect her to offer her opinion?

Michael rose and set her tray on an empty chair, then pushed her to one end of the coffee table. "Bend over, sub. We're going to conduct an experiment."

No way. If she bent over, they'd—

All three doms frowned at her hesitation. *Oh Crom.* She obeyed and tried to reassure herself that Michael wouldn't do anything horrible. *I want Master Simon here.*

"Hands flat on the coffee table, Rona."

She did, all too aware of how her coat didn't cover her butt. But at least she stood sideways to the two men in the chairs; they wouldn't see it. She dropped her head and closed her eyes. Now what?

"Look at Logan and Jake," Michael said.

Okay. Both men watched her with that focused dom look.

"Now don't move, sub." Michael swept his hands up and down

her legs. Then his fingers brushed behind her knees, tickling until she wiggled. He laughed and moved his hand up to the tender skin just below her bottom, caressing it. Not a tickle now. Her lips compressed as pleasure ran through her.

"Jake wins," Logan announced, and a grin flashed in his leathery face.

"My turn." Jake stood, tall and muscular. As Michael seated himself, the other dom walked behind her. God, looking right at her butt, dimples and—

His hand caressed the crease below her bottom, touching and grazing until she could feel her thong turn damp. When he slid his hand down to stroke behind her knee, she sighed in relief.

"Sorry, Michael. That's two for two," Logan said. "Looks like, on this sub at least, below the ass beats the knee area."

"In my opinion, that spot wins every time." Jake slapped her bare butt lightly, startling her, and took his seat again.

Were they done? Could she move now?

"There's one more theory to consider." The rich timbre of the voice from just behind Rona made every muscle in her body contract. *Master Simon.*

She turned her head, trying to see him, and got a stinging swat on her bottom. "Don't move, sub."

Her jaw clenched, and yet heat seemed to stream off her as if from a raging forest fire.

"And what's your theory, Simon?" Logan asked.

"That with the right dom, a touch anywhere is erotic."

The men grinned at each other. Michael said, "Perhaps you should demonstrate."

Rona strained her ears. Nothing.

"Now, lass." His voice seemed to caress her, despite the stern authority in it. "Don't move. Keep your eyes on the other doms."

A quiver ran through her, and she forced herself to stay still. A moment passed. Another. He stood right behind her. She could feel his warmth and his gaze on her exposed bottom.

His fingers grazed over her ankle. She pulled in a ragged breath at the sensation and the knowledge that this was *Simon's* touch. A moment later, his hard hand closed around her calf and squeezed, and somehow the warmth of his skin and the slight scrape of his callous fingers sent electricity sizzling straight to her clit so fast that she had to force down a moan.

The doms burst out laughing.

Jake shook his head. "Always some bastard screwing up a good experiment."

A low chuckle sounded behind her, and Rona stiffened. What was he going to do?

"But I have to say, Jake," Master Simon said, "I also prefer the just-below-the-ass spot." A pause and then his hand traced the crease between her thigh and bottom with one...deliberate...stroke. Warm, rough, firm.

No longer under her control at all, her hips pressed back against his touch.

Master Simon's laugh was deep and masculine. "Up you come, lass. Experiment's over." He gripped her arm and helped her stand. With a shock, she realized his other hand hadn't moved and now cupped her buttock. He squeezed slightly.

Her legs shook as she looked up at him, feeling the strength in the ruthless grip on her arm, keeping her right beside him so he could touch her as he pleased. His fingers stroked over her bottom, slowly, and each movement increased her arousal.

When he finally released her, satisfaction glimmered in his eyes. He touched her cheek gently. "Do you know how lovely you are when you're aroused, sweetheart?"

He tilted his head at the other doms. "Thank you, gentlemen, for allowing me to participate," he said and strode away.

As Rona tried to get her breathing under control, the doms exchanged glances. "Well, that seemed clear enough," Jake drawled. "You ever see Simon get territorial before?"

"Should be an interesting evening." Logan pulled his fair-skinned sub between his knees, and the pretty sub's eyes closed in pleasure as he played with her hair. A wistful envy ran through Rona. What would it be like to sit at a man's feet, to feel his— Master Simon's—hands on her?

"Not for me, apparently," Michael grumbled.

Rona frowned. Had she missed something?

Michael handed over her tray of drinks and smiled at her. "Off you go, pet."

By the time she'd emptied the drink tray, she'd grown— almost—used to being on display. The excitement that Master Simon had roused hadn't dissipated at all. The sights and sounds of people making love, of floggers and groans and whimpers, kept her in a pure state of need. Three doms had asked her to play, all interesting and pleasant men, so why had she said no?

Because she'd gotten fixated on Master Simon. Just like now, each time she spotted him, her whole body seemed to jump up and down, screaming, *Him, him, him.*

She set the tray down and leaned against the living-room wall. After all the lectures she'd given herself, and the goals she'd posted on the bulletin board, she was still being stupid about a man.

Chapter Six

AH, THERE SHE was. Simon spotted his little sub leaning against the wall just outside the kitchen. He'd kept an eye on her—she continued to refuse other doms. Good. Watching her with someone else would hurt like hell. He wanted to be the one to show her more, to bring her to orgasm. He wanted her trust...and more.

Gently, though. She'd take flight too easily.

First the bait. He set his bag beside the high recliner-style table, one of his favorites, with extra width and leather padding. One by one, he pulled the vacuum cups out of his bag and lined them up on a paper towel on a nearby coffee table.

The sub he'd commandeered in the kitchen set down a pan of bleach water. "Ooooh, Master Simon, you're going to do cupping?"

He nodded. When he turned, he saw Rona join the people gathering around the table. If she wanted variety and exploration, he'd be happy to fulfill that need. He captured her gaze. "Come here, lass."

A SHAKING STARTED in Rona's stomach at the smoky growl of Master Simon's voice. Then the words registered. *"Come here."*

"Me?" Her voice squeaked.

"You." He rolled up one sleeve, looked over at her, and frowned. "Now."

Oh no. She needed to think, but her feet moved her forward. Her hands went numb, and yet desire sizzled through her with each step closer. Her skin felt sensitive, the brush of her Santa coat like sandpaper. When she met his intent, measuring eyes, her chest squeezed as if he had her ribs between his big hands.

She stopped in front of him.

"Good girl." He cupped her chin in one hard hand. "Such big eyes." He brushed his mouth across hers and released her.

"I-I…" What had she planned to say?

"Remember the rules about speaking, little sub." He patted the table. "I want you on here—without the coat."

The people. She didn't have anything on but that skimpy bra and thong. Her eyes met his.

"You've watched all night but haven't played…and you want to, Rona." He ran a finger down her cheek, his smile just for her. "I'll go slowly, little one."

A tremor ran through her. *I want to do this. And I want to do this with him.*

He waited patiently, but his confident posture said he already knew her answer. How could that feel so reassuring?

She pulled off her coat and handed it to him, shivering at the feeling of air—and eyes—against her skin.

"Good girl." The approval in his dark eyes warmed her. He grasped her around the waist and set her on the countertop-high table, then swung her legs up.

The slick leather chilled her bottom, and she clenched her hands in her lap.

"Now, tell me. Do you want to watch or just feel?"

She bit her lip and stared at the clear glass cups, which suddenly seemed a little ominous. "Watch."

"All right." He adjusted the table to lean her back in a reclining position. Before she could object, he tugged open the ribbons on her bra and pulled it off.

Great. Baby-chewed breasts with white stretch marks. She

forced her hands to stay in her lap and not cover them.

To her surprise, his eyes held only appreciation as he looked at her for a long, long moment. When his callous hands finally cupped her breasts, her back arched. Somehow she felt as if she'd been waiting for his touch all night. His thumbs traced circles around her nipples, and heat pooled in her pelvis.

"I can see I won't have to warm you up very much," he murmured. He leaned down and took her mouth, even as his hands moved over her breasts, teasing and playing until the world rippled around her. He pulled back to smile at her. "I don't know when I've enjoyed kissing someone so much. You give everything you have, sweetheart."

And he kissed her again, a sweet kiss that turned forceful, his tongue taking complete possession.

When he stopped, she couldn't move, could only stare up into his intent gaze. Why did surrendering to this man feel so right?

After studying her, he nodded and said softly, "That's my sub." And the utter assurance in his claim terrified her when she couldn't find any disagreement inside her.

He picked up a strap and buckled it just below her breasts. A softly lined cuff went on each wrist, and he secured them to the top of the table over her head. Then he walked to the foot of the table.

She eyed him nervously, again aware of the people watching. "What are—"

His stern glance strangled the words in her throat. *Silence. Don't talk. But...*

Her knees bent as he pushed her feet upward toward her butt. Then he restrained her ankles to the edges of the table, the position far too like the one her gynecologist used, only even more spread open—the width of Simon's table was twice that of a medical one.

She pulled on her arms and legs, suddenly feeling frighteningly helpless.

"Ah, lass." He walked back and held her face between his hands. She looked into his eyes. Calm and confident.

"Nothing will happen that you won't enjoy, Rona. If you become too scared, you can use your safe word. Tell me what it is."

She swallowed. His thumbs stroked her cheeks as he waited for her answer.

"Houston. It's Houston."

"That's right, my lass." He held her head between his hands as he enjoyed her mouth in a leisurely kiss, as if he had all night, as if people weren't waiting for him.

When he let her go, her resistance had melted away. The knowledge that right now she'd submit to anything he wanted chilled her a little. Master Simon knew exactly what he was doing, and she wasn't sure if she resented or admired his power.

He looked into her eyes and smiled. "Thinking again?"

She watched him walk toward the end of the table, and every one of those eased muscles started to tighten again. When he undid the laces of her thong and pulled it off, a sizzle of excitement shot through her system. Her moan almost sounded like a whimper.

His eyes crinkled. He didn't touch her, though, and she was glad—really—although everything down there throbbed in need.

"Let's start with your nipples," he said. He picked up a small glass, bell-shaped cup and set it against her left breast. The coolness drew her nipple tighter. Shaking his head, he chose another size and fastened something that looked like a caulking gun with a gauge to the pointed end of the glass.

Unexpectedly, he skimmed his hand over her pussy, making her gasp. "Nice and wet," he said. He ran his now-damp fingers around the glass rim before pressing it firmly to her breast. "Ready, lass?"

Her body burned with arousal even as anxiety shot through her. She gave him a nod and stared down at her chest.

"Tell me if it starts to hurt. For now, you are permitted to speak." He squeezed the handle.

One pump and her breast felt like someone was sucking on it really, really hard. Her nipple swelled into the bottom third of the clear cup. "Oh my God!"

He chuckled, his gaze intent on her face as he squeezed again. When the suction increased to near pain, she tried to push the cup away and rediscovered that she was restrained.

"That's obviously enough." He twisted the pump off, leaving her nipple fat and red inside the vacuum cup. "Next."

The other one went the same way.

"That looks so strange," she muttered, staring at the cups on her breasts. *Feels strange too. Like someone constantly sucking right there.*

He walked to the end of the table, and her hands clenched into fists. Her legs were splayed wide, her pussy on view for everyone to see. And he was going to do...that to her. Her breathing sped up again, yet somehow the fear only increased her arousal.

He ran his finger over her folds, smiling as her hips jerked. "You're very wet."

After being aroused all evening, she felt swollen and almost too sensitive when he slid a finger into her. *Oh God.* Her legs quivered, but the ankle cuffs kept her from moving. Watching her face, he thrust in and out with excruciating slowness, ramping up her burning need. Her hips strained upward. *More, more, more.*

A corner of his mouth curved upward in a smile. "I believe you're ready for the next step."

He picked up a cup, twisted on the pump, and then seated the cold glass firmly around her clit, wiggling to get an adequate seal.

Oh God, she was really going to let him do this. The restraints, his hard hands, his control, the strange cups... She bit her lip, feeling more aroused than she'd ever been in her whole life.

His fingers flexed on the trigger.

Sucking and pressure and tightness. "Oooh." Her hips strained upward, and her eyes closed as the shocking sensation blasted through her. The vacuum increased until her swollen tissue throbbed in time with her pulse.

"Look, Rona." He twisted off the pump, leaving the cup on her clit.

She stared down. Pink flesh half filled the cup, pressing up against the sides. "That's me?"

"Oh yes." He tapped the cup with a finger, and she jumped at the zing of pleasure. "It will remain that size for quite a while after I remove the cup." His eyes glinted at her. She tried not to imagine his fingers on her clit afterward.

"How long do the cups stay on?" She should have asked more questions before starting this maybe.

"Oh, awhile yet."

And she'd just sit here and stare at them?

"Don't worry; I'm not going to let you get bored."

The crowd around rippled in laughter.

SIMON SMILED AS Rona's blue-green eyes showed her arousal—and her anxiety. With her body open and exposed, bound for whatever he wanted to do to it, she displayed her trust in him—trust he hadn't yet earned, but that she'd given him freely, without logic or reason.

Yet he wanted more than her arousal, more than her trust.

"What are you—"

He interrupted her. "Unless you're answering a question, I want you silent now, pet."

She bit her lip, and a tremor ran through her as her worry and arousal both increased. Lovely. How would she deal with additional stimulation? With pain? He picked up a thin cane from his toy bag. "Remember your safe word?"

"Yes." When he lifted an eyebrow, she hastily added, "Sir."

"Excellent." He brushed the thin wood across her ankle, up her calf. He glided the tip over her pussy beneath the cup, up her torso to spiral around the cups on her breasts, and then back down.

Her stomach muscles quivered under the teasing strokes. Her gaze was fixed on the stick.

He lifted it and tapped her thigh lightly. She startled, and the movement wiggled the cups. He could almost see the sensation break through her like a wave. *Very nice.* He struck softly then, up and down one thigh, moved to the other, continuing until the skin pinkened and her hips strained upward.

Her eyes slowly took on the glazed look of a submissive over-whelmed by sensation and endorphins.

He removed a glass dildo from his bag, wet it in her juices, and slid it in.

AHHH! RONA JERKED back to awareness as every nerve in her pussy shocked to life. She tried to move, couldn't, and her breathing sped up. She'd been drifting as the rhythmic sensations of pain from the cane somehow merged with the aching feeling from the cups and sent her somewhere else.

But now the dildo tightened the skin around her clit, her vagina throbbed, and each beat of her pulse pushed her closer to coming. Her eyes closed as she shivered.

"Look at me, Rona." His darkly masculine voice caressed her as surely as his warm hand on her face.

She opened her eyes. God, he was so gorgeous, like a blade, but not a bland kitchen knife—more like a medieval dagger. Elegant and deadly, but the look in his eyes was so caring. Almost loving. She smiled.

"There, that's better." He patted her cheek. "Keep your eyes on me, lass. And by the way, you do not have permission to come."

It took a minute for the meaning of his words to percolate through the molasses in her brain. *Not come?* "But—"

"No. No coming." His grin flashed. He stepped back and brushed that wicked, thin cane across her breast and then struck the side.

Unh! The sting echoed through her breast. He slapped the cane harder, circling around the cups on her breasts. Each sharp pain knifed through her, and yet all she could process was the thick intrusion in her vagina and the squeezing of her clit. She tried to wiggle, but the straps over her ribs held her implacably in place. And each erotically painful blow increased the coiling inferno inside her, brought her closer to coming.

"Oh pleeeeease." The moan broke from her. "I need—"*Need to come, need just a little more.*

He stopped.

Panting, she stared up at him, trying to order her thoughts.

He closed his warm hand over her restrained ones. "Now, sweetheart, you have two choices. I can bring you off here and now...or you can join me upstairs, and we can make love."

"Have sex?"

His eyes darkened, and he repeated, "We can make love."

The phrasing didn't sound right, but oh God, just the thought of his hands on her... She shivered and whispered, "You."

His gaze lingered on her face. Then he brushed a kiss over her lips. "You please me more than I can say, Rona." He released the vacuum on the cups and popped them off, one by one. The dildo slid out, leaving her empty and aching. He tossed everything in a nearby pan of water.

Rona stared at her body, shocked at her red, hugely swollen nipples. And her clit... Tripled in size, it blatantly pushed out from between her labia. Aching. Tight. Needy.

He undid the restraints and set her in a chair while he swiped down the table with a paper towel and spray. "Feel free to use the cupping toys," he told the people still gathered. "Logan, Jake, can you monitor the place for a bit?"

"Abandoning his own party," Jake said to his brother in mock disapproval. "Sure, Simon. We'll babysit for you."

After tucking her into her Santa coat, Master Simon took Rona upstairs and down a hallway to the master bedroom. A gas fireplace flickered to life, sending shadows dancing on the walls. The rich blue carpet under her feet was thick enough to wade through; dark wood furniture gleamed in the dim light.

"I've had visions of you in my bed," he murmured, stripping the coat off her. "And of making love with you."

He lifted her and put her in the center of his bed, forcing her onto her back with a merciless strength that made her mind whirl. When he pulled her arms over her head, she remembered he hadn't removed her wrist or ankle cuffs. A sharp *click* and he'd hooked her wrist cuffs to a single chain attached to the headboard. She yanked at the chain, a tremor running through her. Alone with a man she barely knew. And she'd let him restrain her. Was she insane?

"Relax, pet," he murmured, brushing her lips with his. "We will both enjoy this, or we won't continue. Say, 'Yes, Master.'"

Why did just the sound of his low voice make her muscles loosen? Why did she trust him like this? She inhaled, then frowned. Say what? "Master?"

A satisfied smile lightened his chiseled features. "That's the word. Say it again."

She hesitated. When his strong hands cupped her breasts and pressed them together, the devastating sensation turned her willpower to mush. "Master." But as she said the word, everything inside her tightened in denial…and yet the oddest sense of contentment filled her, as if the last piece of a jigsaw puzzle had snapped into place.

"That's right." Still standing beside the bed, he kissed her slowly, his tongue possessing her mouth as thoroughly as his hands took her breasts. He drew back. As she tried to recover her swirling senses, he pushed a pillow under her bottom.

He stripped easily and unself-consciously, but the sight of him stole her air. His muscular forearms had hinted at his build but hadn't prepared her for the wideness of his chest, solid with muscle. Black hair dusted over his pectorals and spiraled to his groin as if to showcase his cock.

Her breath turned ragged. He was maybe a little longer than normal, yes, but the width… As if to tantalize, dark veins twisted around the incredibly thick shaft. He followed her gaze and chuckled. "Yes, I've been erect since you walked in this evening, and I look forward to taking you," he said softly. "But I intend to play with you first. To love you."

His hands kneaded her breasts gently. "Have I mentioned how beautiful these are?" He smiled into her eyes before lowering his head. His mouth closed over her nipple, and the sensation of heat and wetness around the still-puffy tissue made her head spin. He swirled his tongue across the peak, then pushed her breasts upward, tightening the skin, increasing the pleasure as he suckled hard. When his lips closed on her other nipple, the sensation ripped straight to her clit so intensely, it verged on the edge of painful. Her nipples contracted to fat, aching points.

And then he moved onto the bed, parting her legs. He settled between her thighs and...looked at her down there.

The excitement of being on display warred with embarrassment, and she jerked at her arms. She couldn't move. She tried to put her legs together, but he was in the way. He gripped her knees and ruthlessly pushed them back out—even farther than before. Cool air brushed over her wet pussy as her folds opened.

"Rona, either keep your legs apart—just like this—or I will restrain them. Which?"

Right now, the thought of added bondage seemed more scary than exciting. "I'll behave. Sir."

"Good. I enjoy watching you struggle to obey." His hands grazed up her inner thighs to the very edge of her pussy, and his thumbs pulled her outer labia more open, exposing her fully. He bent, and his tongue slid through her folds, dancing up and down, tracing patterns around her entrance, before finally moving up to the aching center of nerves.

That huge clit. She was so aroused that the throbbing there felt like torture. She barely had time to wonder how being licked would feel when he took it completely into his mouth. Devastating pleasure blasted through her. "Oh Lord!"

Her hips lifted uncontrollably. His hands pressed her flat, giving her no chance to move, and then he blew lightly on her clit.

The coolness tensed it further, and her legs shook. A whine escaped her.

His tongue circled the puffy ball of flesh, and her stomach clutched at the electrifying feeling.

"Your clit is here"—he touched it, and the startling sensation made her jump—"and the hood is all the way back here." Another light touch.

She moaned. He spread her moisture around and over the nub, each leisurely stroke an exquisite torment.

"It's so far out that I can tug on it." His thumb and fingers closed, and each tiny pull just intensified the sensation. *More, oh, please, more.* She bent her knees and pushed her hips up.

He slapped her thigh. The stinging pain shocked through her, and yet her clit pulsed even more fiercely.

"You will stay in place, sub." The low growl set her heart to pounding. "And you will take everything I give you."

His mouth replaced his fingers. Oh God, so hot. His tongue swirled around her clit, rubbing one side and the other, ruthlessly driving her up. Her head tipped back as every muscle in her body tightened…and held.

And then he sucked.

A blinding explosion ripped into her, great, shuddering spasms. She screamed. He didn't stop. Instead he mercilessly teased her nub with light flicks of his tongue, sending waves of pleasure reverberating through her system.

When he finally granted her mercy, she groaned. Her heart pounded so violently, her chest felt bruised from the inside, and a fine sweat covered her body. Nothing had ever felt like this before. She opened her eyes and stared at him.

His cheek creased as he smiled at her. "You come beautifully, but a little too fast." He nipped the inside of her thigh, and her vagina clenched. "I'll make you work for the next one, lass."

Next one? She wasn't the insane one; he was.

With strong hands, he flipped her over and onto her bent knees. When she tried to rise, he dragged her down the bed until her arms straightened, stretched toward the headboard.

She dropped her head to rest on her upper arm. "Simon?"

"Who?"

Her insides quaked at his icy voice. Just as he'd exposed her most intimate parts, this demand seemed to open hidden caverns inside her, spilling her secrets of need. Of desire. But he'd already known...known that she wanted this, wanted him to do whatever he desired. She'd been the one in denial. But that word he wanted her to say demanded even more of her than just exposure. No. "Sir, what are you doing?"

His hands ran over her body, firm and possessive, placing her for his pleasure. "Rona, I'm going to take you now."

She heard the crinkling of a condom wrapper, and her muscles stiffened in anticipation.

His cock pressed against her, and he stroked the head in her wetness, sending a shiver of hunger through her. Then he entered her with a steady, unyielding push.

She was very wet, and despite that, her body tried to resist as her vagina stretched around the unaccustomedly large intrusion. But oh sweet heavens, he felt good, filling the emptiness inside her.

Of course, she'd not get off this time, but how cool that she'd climaxed even once this first time together. She'd enjoy it when he got off.

He chuckled and squeezed her bottom. "Thinking again, lass?" Only halfway in, now he pulled back, and the friction stroking through her folds sent tension riding up her spine. He pushed in faster, then in and out, farther with each thrust, until his hips rubbed against her bottom. The startling fullness squeezed her swollen clit, and it throbbed with building desire.

She wiggled her hips, moving him inside her, and he laughed. "Still too much mobility, I see. Next time, I'll hog-tie you." The image sent a thrill through her.

"But for now, we'll do it this way." He pushed her lower legs apart, until she balanced precariously on her widespread knees. As he massaged her bottom, the movements made him slide inside her and sent zings of fire through her. Her inability to resist upped the intensity in a frightening way.

"Good," he murmured in satisfaction, and his hands secured her hips, anchoring her completely as he started to move. Out, in. Gently, then harder, pulling her back on her haunches to meet his hard thrusts. She struggled in his grip as her excitement steadily rose, and his merciless possession fueled the fire until each thrust sent flares of pleasure through her. Her mind hazed as need built to the explosion point. She clenched around him, nerves screaming, hovering on the precipice.

And then he leaned forward, his chest hot against her back, as he supported himself on one arm. His free hand slid around to her front, and she felt his fingers slide through her folds, finding her sensitive, swollen clit. He rubbed one side as his thick cock thrust into her, rubbed the other side with another thrust. He didn't stop, even as uncontrollable tremors shook her.

Her puffy flesh engorged, becoming so taut and sensitive that she moaned with each touch of his fingers. One more...harder... Something...to make her come. Her trembling legs strained to lift her to his cock...or lower her to his hand—she didn't know what she wanted.

More. "Please," she whimpered.

"Please what, love?" His voice, intense, unbending. His rough jaw scraped her shoulder. His touch and thrusts never slowed.

Please do more, please... Not the words he demanded. "Master," she whispered. "Please."

"Nothing would please me more than to fulfill your request." He leaned back, balanced on his knees. His palm compressed her mound as his fingers opened her folds widely, increasing the pressure on her clit. As he rammed into her, hard and fast, the slickened fingers of his other hand slid up and down her clit, plucking it gently. Up and down, thrust, up and down, thrust. Everything inside her coiled tighter and tighter, her hips tried to move, to get... He gripped her mercilessly, forcing her to take only what he wanted to give her. *Up and down.* Suddenly his cock angled and hit something incredibly sensitive inside her.

Her neck arched back, and then her climax surged upward from her pelvis, a volcanic eruption of heat and pleasure, one explosion after another until even her fingertips tingled. "*Oh, oh, oh!*"

She bucked against his strong arms, and he held her in place, forcing her to take more as he stroked her gently, inside and out.

Her head dropped onto her arm as she gasped for breath, the tremors easing. She'd never…never come like that, been so lost to everything. Tears burned her eyes as he kissed her neck, murmuring how beautiful she was, how much she pleased him. Her breathing slowed as he soothed her like a nervous filly.

When she slumped, his arms flexed, keeping her up. "Not quite yet, pet."

His hands moved to clasp her hips. He pumped into her in short, powerful strokes and then thrust deep. She had only a second to feel his cock jerking inside her with his release, and then he squeezed her swollen clit. She screamed as another explosion shook her very foundation.

HER PUSSY MILKED the last spasm out of his cock like a hot fist, even as the little sub's shoulders flattened onto the bed. Her hair spilled over her arms, and her skin was a creamy white against the royal blue of the bed quilt. She was utterly beautiful in her surrender. He remained in place for a moment, savoring the tiny shudders that rippled through her body at intervals, before pulling out. He quietly used the bathroom to remove the condom.

She hadn't moved when he returned. After unclipping the chain—she looked so pretty in cuffs that he left them on—he lay down beside her and gathered her against his side, settling her head in the hollow of his shoulder. With a soft sigh, she snuggled into him like a well-fed kitten, draping an arm across his chest and a leg over his thigh.

Cuddly and responsive, smart and submissive. He'd known her such a short time, and yet she filled the emptiness inside him. He wanted to keep her. Right here. In his bed.

In his home.

He rubbed a hand up and down her back. A few seconds later she patted his chest and stroked him in return. As thoroughly as he'd used her and as she'd come, her body must be as exhausted as her mind—yet she still tried to give something back. The woman warmed his heart, and his arm pulled her closer. Damned if he'd let her go.

Unlike a relationship that moved gradually from friendship into love, his feelings for Rona had bloomed suddenly, like the mountain wildflowers of his birthplace. Even at first, Rona hadn't seemed like a stranger. He'd known her. Much like when he'd arrived in San Francisco and something inside him had said, *This place. I belong here.*

He felt the same with Rona. *She belongs here. With me.*

As she snuggled against him, he touched one breast, smiling at the still-puffy, reddened nipple. When he plucked the velvety peak, he felt the sensation jolt through her. Yes, the way she responded to him, to his voice and his body, said that part of her acknowledged the tie. But her practical brain wouldn't accept something so illogical.

She was a stubborn woman. He admired that. *Dammit.* She'd set her course and wasn't the type to lightly turn aside. Made a dom want to bring out the flogger.

Chapter Seven

RONA'S HEAD RESTED on Simon's shoulder, and under her hand on his chest, his heart beat with slow thuds. The room smelled of sex and his subtle cologne. When he pulled her closer, she let him, needing that comfort as a barrier against the lost feeling creeping through her. The knowledge of how alone she'd be in a few minutes. When he let her go.

That just didn't make any sense. She'd just had good—no, fantastic—sex, but now... She blinked back the tears stinging her eyes.

His arm around her tightened, and his free hand caressed her cheek. "Lass—"

"We need to get up," she interrupted quickly, her voice husky. He knew. And she didn't want to talk about it. About anything.

His hand paused, and his chest rose and fell in a silent sigh. "All right. I am the host, I suppose." He stroked her hair back behind her ear. "But we will talk of what is troubling you later."

The gentleness and yet the determination in his voice made her eyes burn again. Why did he have to be so...so perfect? Damn him. He'd already sucked her into wanting him, despite her vow to find other men first. She'd never felt like this before. *I belong here.* The thought sparked her to moving—she'd been comfortable with her husband too, and look how that had turned out.

So maybe she hadn't found Mark as totally hot or been taken so thoroughly or come so hard—twice—or... *Crom, can I get more illogical?* She pushed herself up and off the bed. "Well, um, thank you for a great time."

Still sprawled on the bed, Simon put his arms behind his head and watched her with a quiet, steady gaze. "You are quite welcome."

"I'm going back downstairs now." She needed to find someone to help her get her mind off this…overwhelming man. She pulled on the Santa coat, wishing for the damned belt to hold it shut. Hopefully her bra and thong were still in the living room.

"For speaking and trying to leave without permission, you are fined your underwear," Simon said, his voice level, without a hint of humor. "You may continue to wear the coat."

"But—"

"Do you desire to forfeit the coat also?"

She shook her head. But no underwear? She looked down. Oh heavens. Her nipples remained a vivid red, and almost fluorescent in color, her clit still poked out from between her labia. She yanked the coat shut.

Simon rose to his feet. Without speaking, he peeled her coat open and cupped her breasts in his hands. She grabbed his wrists, then dropped her arms when his jaw turned stern. Mercilessly, he teased her nipples into rigid points, continuing until her toes curled into the rug.

"Now you may return downstairs. And, Rona?" He tipped her chin up, forcing her to look at him. "I enjoy seeing your breasts and pussy, and for tonight, I will permit my guests to also share in the sight. So if I see you holding the coat closed, I'll take it from you."

Her throat shut at the look in his eyes. Dark, possessive…heady.

"What do you say to me, sub?"

"Yes, Mas—"*No no no. He isn't.* "Yes, Sir."

His mouth compressed, and she saw the muscle in his jaw flex. "That isn't correct, but I'll let it pass for now. I think you will change your mind, Rona," he said softly, running his finger over her lips.

"No. I won't." She backed away from him and out of the bedroom. *I mustn't.* She remembered the long, boring years of inane conversation, of lying beside her husband, wondering where even the tiny passion they'd shared had gone; the times when they did make love in the missionary position, and if Mark felt greatly daring—or had had a few drinks—from behind.

Yet she couldn't erase the memory of the last hour, Simon's ruthless grip, his fingers teasing her swollen clit. Would sex with him ever be boring?

Maybe, maybe not. She couldn't—wouldn't—take the chance. She owed it to herself to sample everything a single life had to offer.

THE NOISE OF the party burst over her as she reached the bottom of the stairs. Hauling in a breath, she let her coat flap open—*damn the man*—and went to have some more fun.

An hour later she couldn't figure out what had happened with her. The men were wonderful and nice, and she kept saying no to them. Because of *Simon.* She needed to leave. Being near him affected her judgment, no doubt about it.

On the way to the changing room, she walked past a scene in a nook under the stairs. She glanced in and stopped.

Chained to a post, a ball-gagged woman sobbed violently, tears streaming down her face, as a big dom struck her over and over with a thick cane. Angry crimson welts covered the sub's body.

The woman saw Rona, and despite the gag, the word she spoke—"red"—came through clearly enough. *The safe word.*

The dom ignored her. Rona didn't, and she raised her voice so everyone in the area could hear. "Red! She's saying 'red.' Stop right now."

The dom glared over his shoulder. "Get the hell out of my scene, slut." And he turned back, prepared to strike his sub.

Rona took a step forward—damned if she'd stand by—when a steely arm around her waist swung her to one side.

"My job, lass. Thank you for the alert." Master Simon caught the cane on the downswing and wrenched it from the dom. Rona flinched as she realized that the dom was younger, taller than Simon, and outweighed him by at least fifty pounds.

He swung. Simon slapped the beefy arm to one side, stepped in, and buried his fist in the man's gut. The man made a horrible sound and folded forward, clenching his abdomen. Turning slightly, Simon slammed the guy's face into his raised knee. The *crack* of a nose breaking twisted Rona's stomach.

Simon let the moaning man drop to the ground and glanced at the gathered guests. "Logan, would you pack up his bag, please. Jake, drag him out?"

Jake nodded, his face rigid.

"Nice work, buddy," Logan said.

Ignoring the others, Rona headed for the sub. She unstrapped the ball gag and started on the restraints. A second later Simon joined her, working on the other arm.

Once unbound, the sub collapsed, saved from a nasty fall only by Simon's arm around her waist. She had welts all over her body, and she shook so hard her teeth chattered.

Rona scowled at the chilled skin under her hand. She pointed at a sub in the crowd. "Get me a couple of blankets."

She targeted another elf. "I need a hot drink. Coffee, tea, hot chocolate—anything."

"Yes, ma'am." That sub ran for the kitchen even as the other returned with a soft afghan. Rona wrapped the sub in the blanket and followed as Simon carried her out to the living room. Still holding her, he looked around and said, "Jake, she needs a warm body."

One of the rugged brothers had returned. He took the sub and settled onto the couch, cuddling her against him and murmuring in a rumbling voice.

Nice. Rona accepted the hot tea from the sub she'd sent and tested the liquid with a finger. Nice and warm. After sitting beside Jake, she held the cup to the sub's mouth. "Drink, honey."

The sub didn't even seem to hear her.

Jake's big hand closed around the cup, and his voice deepened, darkened. "Little sub."

The sub stiffened in his arms.

"Drink this now."

Rona almost found herself reaching for the cup to obey the forceful command. Instead she shook off the effect, rose, and watched the sub drink the tea obediently. As the young woman's shivers diminished, her head drooped against Jake's shoulder, and he simply snuggled her closer.

Simon draped an additional blanket around the girl, his face still set in hard lines. "I'll speak with her later about safety and choices in doms."

"I'll take care of it, Simon," Jake said. "I saw the asshole earlier, and I didn't like him then. I should have watched him more carefully."

"And I should have checked my guest list more carefully. Let me know if either of you need anything."

Realizing she was gawking and there was nothing else for her to do, Rona started away. Her insides still quivered at the violence, more from the brutality of the dom than Simon's swift and incredibly graceful attack. She shook her head, remembering the effortless punch. Too tall and dark and smooth to be Chuck Norris, but he surely had the same moves. And that unfailing attitude of protectiveness. Crom, that drew her like a magnet.

Dammit, she just kept getting in deeper.

"Rona." Simon's resonant baritone, despite all her self-warnings, still sent a thrill through her, as if her body was tuned to its music.

She turned. "Yes, Sir?"

He walked up to her, stopping close enough she could smell his aftershave and tangy soap. Feel his warmth. She stiffened her spine and looked up.

Dark, dark eyes still holding a trace of anger. Then he smiled, and everything in her stilled as if she'd gotten the first whiff of spring after a long winter. "Lass, you did well. Not only recognizing that the girl needed help, but getting it. And helping her."

She shrugged. "Anyone would have done the same."

"No, sweetheart. You care, *and* you act. Effectively. That's a rare combination."

Dammit, his approval shouldn't please her so. She ignored the warmth glowing in her stomach and changed the subject. "Why didn't you sit with her instead of giving her to Jake? You're..." Comforting. No one could be as comforting and safe as Master Simon.

"Jake is uninvolved."

"But so are you."

His eyes crinkled, and he ran a finger down her cheek, his gaze intent. "I am rapidly becoming involved."

"No!" The loud response burst from her. "I am not getting involved. Not with you or anyone. I will experiment, play, and enjoy all kinds of men. I'm not going to confine myself with just one. Never, ever again."

She turned quickly to escape his reaction and hurried away.

SIMON STARED AFTER her, half inclined to put his fist through something. Maybe a wall. Maybe he'd see if that asshole dom was still outside.

"Well, she made that clear enough." A few feet away, Logan had his arm around his pretty, curvy sub, Rebecca.

"She certainly has no problem with expressing her thoughts," Simon growled.

Rebecca laughed, started to speak, and caught herself. She glanced up at her dom.

"Go ahead, little rebel."

"I don't think she'd be so upset if she didn't want you," Rebecca said. "She reminds me of…well, me. Professional, a little stunned by the BDSM stuff, but liking it." She grinned. "I've seen how she looks for you and watches you and hates that, but she can't help herself."

Logan nodded. "She definitely wants you."

"I know." Simon frowned at the doorway through which his sub had fled. "But she's liable to disappear rather than face it." Her ex was an incompetent bastard who had screwed up his marriage with her and kept her there until she saw involvement as a trap. How to get around that?

"She might insist she's looking for other men, but she hasn't accepted any offers all night," Logan said. "Even Jake struck out. She's yours, my friend. She just won't admit it."

She thinks she wants a ton of men. Simon rubbed his hand on his jaw.

As Rebecca leaned against her dom, she idly stroked her collar. Simon had been at the club the night Logan collared her. Rebecca had arrived first, wanting to see if other doms had the same effect on her as Logan.

When Simon had touched her, he'd known she responded to the dominant in him, but not the man—because her heart belonged to Logan.

Could he tolerate what it would take to show Rona the same? To watch another man dominate her? And if he set this up, he'd have to watch. Maybe see her leave with another man. The muscles of his stomach contracted as if anticipating a full-contact blow.

Logan frowned. "Whatever you're thinking looks ugly."

"Painful as hell," Simon muttered. "Probably not ugly."

He nodded at Logan and his sub and went to secure the St. Andrew's cross. This needed to be as public as possible.

NEEDING A MOMENT to recover, Rona visited the kitchen and downed a glass of wine. On the way out, she spotted Master Simon wiping down the St. Andrew's cross. Obviously he planned to do a scene with one of the subs, and…why that mattered to her… Well, it didn't.

A place deep in her chest started to ache. Probably not a heart attack. Unfortunately. *I really need to go home now.*

Once in the powder room, Rona started getting out her street clothes.

The door opened behind her, and Logan's collared sub walked in. The redhead grinned and said, "There you are. I've been looking for you."

"Is something wrong?"

"Well." The sub's brows drew together. "Not exactly, but… Come on. I'll show you." Without waiting for Rona's answer, she shoved Rona's clothing back in the bag and led the way out. For a submissive, she seemed awfully assertive.

"Is it about that poor girl?" Rona hurried to catch up. The red-head moved amazingly fast, through the foyer and into the great room.

At the sight of Master Simon standing by the cross—with no other sub there—Rona halted and spun to retreat.

"Rona," Master Simon snapped out.

Her feet stopped dead, her hands grew damp, and her heart did that annoying jump-up-and-down-it's-Master-Simon dance. She turned.

He crooked a finger at her. *Come here.*

A wave of longing ran through her, but she shook her head. "I'm not going to do a scene with you."

"Not with me. Come *here.*" His chin lifted just that infinitesimal amount that melted every bone and ounce of resistance in her body. How did he do that?

Feeling like a condemned prisoner heading for the gallows, she walked forward.

"Good." He smiled at her, but the look in his eyes was…different. No smile lurked in the depths.

"What's wrong?" she whispered.

Hands on her shoulders, he pushed her back against the wooden frame and lifted her arm over her head.

Snap.

"Hey!" She yanked at the wrist he'd just restrained to the upper arm of the X. Damn, she'd forgotten she still wore cuffs. Ignoring her struggles, he secured her other arm. "What are you doing?"

"Rona, you insist you want an assortment of men, not just one, but you haven't followed through. I'm going to let you experience the variety you wanted."

The floor seemed to drop out from under her. *Men? Other men?*

Before she could react, he pulled her left leg outward and clipped the ankle cuff to the X-frame's lower leg. The feel of his callous hands sent heat rushing through her.

"Master Simon… No." Her voice came out weak. Totally ineffective, considering he didn't stop.

Without speaking, he anchored her other leg, then tightened the restraints until she couldn't move anything, couldn't do anything except wiggle her hips. He didn't notice as he turned and raised his voice loud enough to echo through the house. "Unattached doms. I've placed a sub on the cross for your pleasure. Her safe word is 'Houston.' Each dom will have three minutes to get an interested response from her, using hands or mouth—no toys. Whoever succeeds may remove her restraints and take her. After that, she goes back on the cross."

"Simon," she hissed. "You can't—"

"Is this not what you said you wanted?" The uncompromising look he gave her said *put up or shut up.*

But…

He touched her cheek with his fingertips. "Remain calm, pet. I'll be off to one side to ensure nothing gets out of hand. You're perfectly safe to enjoy your variety of men."

But...

And he walked away.

Rona's breath hitched inside her throat until it felt as if she'd choke. The room had gone silent, leaving only the harsh swishing of her heartbeat in her ears. She couldn't help but yank on the cuffs, but he'd done a fine job of stringing her up. Of course he would. Master Hotshot Simon. She glared at his broad back and realized his sleeves were rolled down. He wouldn't participate.

Disappointment had a bitter taste.

She looked away from him, and her eyes widened. Every single man at the party must have crowded into the living room, all eyeing her with that assessing, dominant stare. She shut down her first inclination—to yell *Houston* and *get me out of here*—and tried to stay rational.

Only what was rational about sex?

But this was her goal and exactly why she had come to the party. She'd wanted to mess around, but instead she'd focused so hard on damn-him-to-hell *Simon* that she hadn't noticed anyone else. Pretty stupid of her, really, especially since Mr. I'm Getting Involved obviously didn't have a problem handing her off to other men. Her throat tightened, and she swallowed and swallowed again, forcing the ache away.

Get over it, Rona. This is right off your goal list; stick to the plan, girl. She raised her chin. She'd show him how much she'd enjoy every single one of these guys.

And thank him for the treat afterward.

The doms cut cards to pick who went first. One tossed down his winning card and headed for her. Medium height, late twenties maybe. The solid blond looked just fine in his leather pants and black T-shirt.

"Uh. Hi," she offered.

Ice blue eyes met hers. "Be quiet. When I want you to speak, I'll let you know."

Pfft. She frowned. Why did his order tempt her to call him an idiot, but that same command from Simon would have sent funny little chills through her?

He went straight for the kill, one hand settling on her pussy, the other on her breast. She was still sensitive from Simon's attentions and the cupping, and it hurt when this idiot pulled at her nipple. When he massaged her clit, she cringed at the dry discomfort.

When Master Simon announced, "Time," she let her head tip back in relief.

The dom gave her a cold look and stalked away.

The next one was even younger, midtwenties, and serious eye candy.

He had a wide smile as he said, "Mmm, I like what that vacuum pump does." He kissed her softly, and his hand brushed over her breast. *Very nice.* Not painful at all.

He bent and sucked on her nipple. She leaned back, only there was no retreat against the wrongness of the sensation. His hand touched her pussy and—

"Time."

"Hell. That's just not long enough." He licked his fingers and groaned. "Find me later, sweetie, and we'll go at it."

She smiled back at him, not promising anything. His touch had been pleasant, but where was the zing?

"Look at me." The next dom's voice sliced into her thoughts like a scalpel through Kleenex.

Her gaze shot up and into intense blue eyes. The dom named Jake.

"Where's the girl?" Rona asked and winced. *Don't talk.*

When his eyes crinkled, he reminded her of Simon, only her heart stayed put rather than doing somersaults. "A friend of hers took her home. We'll make sure she's all right."

"Oh good."

His big hand cupped her cheek, and he tilted her head up. "You're a pretty sub, sugar. I like you."

"I like you too," she said. He'd cared for that poor sub so

sweetly and—

"Look at me. Right at me, girl." Dom voice—rougher. Her eyes met his, were captured. His hand grazed over her breast, slid down her stomach, and inched slowly toward her mound. And she realized, with each man who touched her, she liked it less and less.

His mouth curved. "That's what I thought," he murmured and leaned forward to say quietly into her ear, "I'd have enjoyed teasing that pretty clit, but it appears you're not going to enjoy anyone's touch except a certain dom's."

She stared at him in dismay. "No."

"Oh yes." His hand slid down over her pussy, and she had to force herself not to pull away. She'd make herself like this.

"Some little subs enjoy a variety; some enjoy just a few special men. And some want only one. Just one master of their own." His fingers stroked her pussy gently as he leaned an arm on one of the uprights and talked to her.

One master. Just one. Master.

"I must say," he said softly, as if he spoke only to himself, "I used to think that way too. Want only one. But I've done that, and it's... If it doesn't work..." He shrugged, and she saw pain smoldering in his eyes.

Oh, honey. Her heart squeezed. To give up on love... "No, Jake, just because once didn't work, you mustn't stop trying."

"Time."

His hand pressed against her clit, still not arousing, as he brushed a kiss over her lips. "Rona, just because once didn't work," he repeated back to her, "you mustn't stop trying."

The look he gave her sliced through her defenses like a surgeon's scalpel.

SIMON CLOSED HIS eyes and exhaled. If he'd had to watch Jake's hands on Rona for one second longer, he'd have broken something. With good control, the something might have been the table; otherwise, the bastard's jaw.

His sub had smiled at Jake. She'd talked to him and hadn't pulled away. Jaw tense enough to ache, Simon reset the small kitchen timer and nodded to the next dom. How much of this could he take?

But if she really desired variety, then he'd see she got it, even if his guts twisted into painful knots. She wanted him; he knew that, but either she'd realize it...or she wouldn't. And if she found someone who turned her on—Simon closed his eyes at the sheer stab of pain—then that would be that. No one ever said life had to be fair or that if you fell hard for a woman, that she must return the favor.

He inhaled and set himself to endure some more.

Chapter Eight

RONA SET HER teeth and endured the next dom's touch on her nipples. He wasn't handsome, but older and very polite. She felt nothing.

"Time."

She got a break as more of the doms cut cards, and Jake's words—her own words—kept circling her mind like one of those tunes that wouldn't leave. "*Just because once didn't work…*"

She'd been married—involved—once. Just once in her life. It hadn't worked. And based on that single instance, she'd decided against risking involvement again. Decided she needed to experience everything she'd missed. But after this assortment of men—and face it, any woman would want a man like Jake—she had to admit she felt nothing from them.

Yet one word from Master Simon sent zings and whistles through her like her body'd turned into an old-fashioned pinball machine. And it was more than just excitement, he *felt* right to her. Like she belonged with him. So why did she stubbornly insist on wanting more men?

How long would she continue to ignore her own feelings?

When the next man approached, she looked him in the eye and said, "Houston."

"What?" He gaped at her.

"I'm finished. Houston. Let me down."

Master Simon walked up with that prowling, always balanced gait of his.

The strange dom told him, "She said Houston."

"I heard." The look Simon gave her held no expression whatsoever.

Was he disappointed in her? She bit her lip and looked away as doubt crawled into her stomach and sent cold tentacles through her chest. Maybe he'd decided this was a good way to find her another guy.

"Scene's over, lads," Simon told the waiting doms. "The sub thanks you for your interest."

Rona nodded and tried to smile at the men, feeling her lips quiver. Her eyes stung. She'd thought Simon wanted her, but the cold way he looked at her now...

"I want down." Her voice shook. *I want my clothes, and I want to leave. First he wants me, and then he doesn't, and—*

Firm fingers grasped her chin, lifting it. "Look at me, Rona."

She looked past him, over his big shoulder. *I will not cry, not for this cold dom who flip-flops like a fish on dry land.*

A soft snort of laugher, then his voice lowered. "Look. At. Me."

Her eyes flashed to his and were caught and pinned in his intent gaze.

"That's better," he murmured. "What is going through that clever brain of yours, lass?" The warm, caressing tone wrapped her in warmth.

She tried to shake her head, and his fingers tightened.

"Answer me."

"You looked so angry."

"And you thought I was angry with you?" One corner of his mouth turned up. "Sweetheart, do you know how difficult it was to watch other men touching you?" His thumb stroked over her lips. "I haven't been possessive of a woman in a very long time, but you do bring that out."

Oh. Relief welled up in her like a bubbling spring. "I didn't like being touched by them."

His lips curved. "I noticed that," he said agreeably. In the same move as Jake's, he leaned an arm next to hers on the upright, obviously prepared to listen as long as she wanted to talk.

"They bored me." She took a breath. "I was bored with my husband too. I blamed it on being with just one man."

He tilted his head. *Go on.*

"Apparently having more men isn't the answer." She smiled at him. The banked heat in his eyes showed he was patiently waiting for her to finish, and then he'd take her. The knowledge set everything inside her to a boil. "You don't bore me, Simon."

His expression chilled, sending both anxiety and arousal sizzling through her. "Who?"

Jake's word—"Master"—slid into her mind and trembled across her heart, but she still couldn't bring herself to say it. "Sir," she offered hastily.

"That's better." His fingers threaded through her hair. "For that, you deserve a reward."

Currents of excitement hummed through her system. Her breasts tingled. He hadn't even touched them, and they tingled. This man—the dom—was definitely the man for her. "Oh?"

"You're in an excellent position for a flogging," he murmured. He wet one finger and circled her nipple. As the dampness cooled, the areola bunched into an aching peak. "How would the tips of a flogger feel against all this tender tissue?"

Even as her eyes widened, she felt the wetness between her legs. Lightning raced up her spine.

"Yes, look at those cheeks turn pink," he said, this dom who saw everything. His hand slid down the same path that Jake's had, and with his black eyes watching her so intently, just his touch made her shudder. He stroked past her mound, through the growing wetness, and up to slide over her sensitive clit. He touched her firmly, then gently, until she whimpered. Her hips tilted forward. *More.*

"No, you will not come yet. Or even very soon," he whispered, biting her earlobe. "First I'm going to tease you with the flogger and with my mouth and then take you, right here on the cross, until you scream so loudly that no man in the place will doubt whose sub you are. And neither will you."

Her breath caught.

The grin that flashed over his face set her heart to thumping before he took her lips in a devastating kiss. He cupped her breast, still puffy from his attentions earlier, and the muscles in his jaw set. "I realize you don't want to jump into any commitments, but it's too late, my practical lass."

"But—" When his eyes hardened, she felt every drop of resistance drain right out of her.

"And as long as we are involved, you will not be sampling a variety pack of men." His grin flashed. "However, I guarantee I will not allow you to be bored, whether we are together a year...or fifty."

Even as she shook her head in a reflexive refusal, she remembered the old woman buying the fortieth-anniversary toy for Henry. Obviously a relationship didn't have to be a trap. Rona could experience the world with just one man.

When Simon started to roll up his sleeves, her mouth went dry. He stepped back, inspecting her body slowly. "Say, 'Yes, Master.'"

Did she want to give him more? Give him everything? Just because he could dominate her? But she wanted him. Just him. Her eyes misted, blurring everything except his face...and his dark eyes, where the tenderness was as obvious as his controlled power. He cared for her. Oh, he really did.

Her heart somersaulted inside her chest, then settled, a solid weight of acceptance.

It was time to write a new five-year plan.

He ran a finger down her chin. "Well, lass?"

"Yes." She smiled and tipped her cheek into his palm. "Yes, my Master."

~ The End ~

Reviews

I adore getting reviews for my books. And as a reader, I rely on y'all's opinions to help me decide which story I should buy next. So…if you get a chance, I'd love if you left a review for *Simon Says: Mine*.

Ready for more? Then try,

Master of the Abyss
Mountain Masters & Dark Haven series: Book 3
Available everywhere

On the mountain, the watcher seeks out evil women. And then they die.

Two years ago, when Jake Hunt uncollared his slave, she committed suicide. Guilt-ridden, he will commit to a woman for one night only, devoting his energy to a mountain lodge that caters to a BDSM crowd.

Kallie Masterson is tough. Unwanted as a child, she worked hard to become a wilderness guide. She's proud of who she is, and hurt that Jake frowns on her for acting like a man.

After rescuing the macho guide from a bar fight, Jake is stunned that the ugly men's clothing hides a warm, responsive woman. A submissive woman. When guide business brings her to the lodge on BDSM night, and she is obviously aroused by the play, Jake takes the little sub right into his world of pain and pleasure. He warns her: one-night-only. But she responds so beautifully—so joyously—under his command, that one night soon becomes two, then three…

Then a missing hiker reminds Jake of his past lover, and he realizes he's become too involved. He pulls back.

Meanwhile, the watcher on the mountain has rendered his verdict: Kallie Masterson is evil. The sentence: Death.

Cherise has done it again!! As if there was ever a doubt. A great mix of love, BDSM and mystery. This story is about learning to trust again, healing old psychological wounds and learning to love.

~ The Romance Reviews

Excerpt from

Master of the Abyss

"FUCKING SON OF a bitch," Kallie snarled. What had hit her? She was lying on her stomach on the damned tavern floor. Rising slightly, she wiped sawdust off her face and gagged at the stench of stale beer. *Whoever hit me is going to die.*

With a grunt, she pushed herself up to a sitting position, and for a second, she would have sworn angels were singing. And then, to her regret, the music descended into the noise of men yelling and Swedish curses as the owner tried to move the fighting outside. She took a breath and waited for the world to stop swirling. She'd still kill whoever had hit her—but maybe later.

"Let's see the damage, sugar," said a deep, rumbling voice. Hard hands closed around her arms, steadying her.

She looked up at a darkly tanned, lean face. Strong jaw with a faint cleft in the chin. Thick brown hair. Cobalt blue eyes. *Jake Hunt.* Oh wonderful—of all the people to see her like this. Kallie tried to pull away.

His grip tightened. "Hold still."

"Let go of me."

Ignoring her, he ran his hands down her shoulders and arms, his eyes intent on her face, his touch gentling when she winced. "Banged your shoulder up some."

"I'm fine." The knowledge that she had Jake Hunt checking her over made her want to sink back to the floor in embarrassment. She tried to shove his hands away with as much success as moving a granite boulder. "I don't need any help, got it?"

"Anything else hurt?"

His gaze ran over her body, and she flushed, acutely conscious of her less-than-hourglass shape—more like a two-legged pear. Scarred face or not, the man could have had any woman in Bear Flat and had dated most of the good-looking ones. She wasn't one of them.

"No, nothing hurts," she muttered.

"Your jaw is bruised." He cupped her cheek with a big hand and tilted her face toward the light. "Did you bang your head? Let's see your eyes."

"I said I'm fine." Averting her eyes from his intense gaze, she tried to push his hand away again. Unsuccessfully.

His voice roughened. "Look at me, Kallie."

The low, commanding tone shook her bones, and she shivered. Her gaze flashed up involuntarily.

His eyes narrowed, becoming more intent until she felt like a deer trapped by a cougar. She swallowed hard.

A smile flickered over his angular face. "Well now," he murmured. "Appearances can be deceiving, can't they? Aren't you supposed to be tougher than any man around?" His hand still gentle on her cheek, he ran a thumb over her lips, sending a tremor through her, followed by a wave of heat.

Wimp. Wuss. Her muscles had turned to water, but she managed to grasp his wrist, trying not to notice the thick bones, the steely tendons. She firmed her voice, and it still came out sounding all girlie and weak. "Don't."

"Don't what?" he asked softly. And he regarded her...differently...in a way that sizzled straight to the center of her body.

"Don't look at me like that," she muttered and pushed his hand away.

Amusement lit his eyes, and a corner of his mouth turned up, creasing his cheek. "Oddly enough, I think I like looking at you."

"Oh sure you do. So are you the one who hit me?"

"I don't hit women," he growled…and then his lips quirked up. "There are much better ways to punish sassy wenches."

At the assessing look he gave her, she could feel her face flame red.

"That's a fine color on you, sugar," he murmured and grasped her upper arms, lifting her to her feet as if she weighed no more than a doll. As the room did a fast merry-go-round, Kallie sagged.

He put an iron-hard arm around her waist to keep her upright. She'd had dreams of having his arm around her, but somehow they'd never included being knocked sprawling in a bar first.

"Hey, Kallie." Barney poked his head in the entrance, eliciting a stream of curses from the grizzled Swede who owned the tavern. "I'm sorry. I threw him at the door, not at you."

"You hit me with a person?" When they'd played baseball in high school, Barney's aim had been notoriously bad; it obviously hadn't improved any. After a second, she laughed and shook her head—*whoa, not a good move.* "It's okay. I'm fine."

Giving his gap-toothed smile, Barney disappeared back out the door, and his roar of battle glee drifted in with the night air.

"Nice of you to forgive him," Jake said as he guided her to a chair. When he stepped away, the warmth of his hands still lingered on her waist.

"He's too big to kill easily."

Jake's laugh sent chills across her skin. When her friends surrounded her and their perfume smothered his clean, masculine scent, Kallie felt relieved. Mostly.

"Girl, I can't believe you're all right. You landed really bad." Gina swooped her hands to demonstrate Kallie's dive and face-plant.

Great. Bet he found that just hilarious.

His grin confirmed her opinion, and then he slid a finger down her cheek. "You know, little sprites shouldn't be fighting."

From anyone else in the world, she might have found the remark amusing. From him, after wanting him for so long, it simply hurt. Trying to ignore the way her skin tingled in the wake of his touch, she gave him a cold look. "I'm not little, and I'm not a sprite. Thanks for the help—now go away."

"You're welcome. *Sprite.*" He glanced at his watch, winced, and shot a stern look at her friends. "Someone take her home." Before anyone could respond, he walked away.

As he left the bar, Gina sniffed. "Such a shame that bossy looks so good on him." She patted Kallie's shoulder. "Let me get my purse, and I'll drive you home. You really—"

"I really need a beer," Kallie interrupted. "No, two beers. And a burger and fries. I just got back from a week in the backcountry, and I'm not running home because some pushy"—*gorgeous*—"person"—*bastard*—"thinks I should."

She'd watched her friends turn all syrupy whenever Jake Hunt touched them. Now she'd done the same thing—and she didn't like it one bit.

Also from Cherise Sinclair

Masters of the Shadowlands (contemporary)
Club Shadowlands
Dark Citadel
Breaking Free
Lean on Me
Make Me, Sir
To Command and Collar
This Is Who I Am
If Only
Show Me, Baby
Servicing the Target

Mountain Masters and Dark Haven (contemporary)
Master of the Mountain
Simon Says: Mine (novella)
Master of the Abyss
Master of the Dark Side (novella)
My Liege of Dark Haven
Edge of the Enforcer
Master of Freedom

The Wild Hunt Legacy (paranormal)
Hour of the Lion
Winter of the Wolf

Standalone books
The Starlight Rite (Sci-Fi Romance)
The Dom's Dungeon (contemporary)

A WILDer Kind of Love

Book 7 in Angel Payne's

W.I.L.D. Boys of Special Forces Series

Coming June 16, 2015

Pre-order available now

Sneak-Peek Preview

The WILD Boys are back. USA Today Bestseller Angel Payne continues the hotter-than-hot series with this sensual, emotional story featuring CIA special agent Daniel Colton.

A scarred hero...

Dan Colton was once the CIA's golden boy, a get-things-done cowboy who believed forgiveness was better to ask for than permission. But performing the devil's work was always easy with his angel's face, a damn good asset to have whether he was charming agency superiors...or training submissives in his darkest dungeon role plays.

Until his face was taken away.

An act of ultimate bravery has spit Colton back out as a bitter, burned shell of the person he used to be, unsure of how to relate to the world without his physical calling card. His only condolence is dreaming of revenge on the bastard responsible for the fire that disfigured him, but when even that plan backfires, he is a beast without any prey—tormented by a beauty he cannot touch.

A willing submissive...

Wyn Lesange, known around the CIA's Vegas office as "The Laser", has only one Achilles heel—in the form of the brooding agent who once wouldn't give her the time of day. Since Dan Colton's accident, they've become friends, even trusting each other with some of their kinkier secrets. What are friends for, right?

Wrong.

A dangerous masquerade...

Now Dan has become her greatest joy, toughest torment, and most sinful desire. Thoughts of surrendering to his passionate brand of domination consume her more and more...but it's clear Dan thinks of her as nothing more than the brainy analyst in the next office over.

Seeking to assuage her need for the submissive dream, Wyn takes matters into her own hands and journeys in disguise to one of the desert's most elicit kink clubs. When the Dominant she meets there is also beneath a mask, his voice so alluring and familiar, she wonders if karma has conspired to fulfill one of her deepest fantasies...and what price she'll have to pay for it come true. Is she willing to sacrifice everything she's built in a friendship with Dan, for one night in his dungeon?

Excerpt

"LITTLE ROSE."

Tess jumped out of her chair. Literally. Not that it had been a particularly comfortable chair. She'd found another wingback in the second of Catacomb's living room areas, hoping she'd have better results in here at the whole calm-down-and-talk-to-somebody-dammit efforts.

And did all that go for you, missie? Did changing rooms help you escape one drop of the feeling that you've showed up at Prom without a date, three damn nights in a row?

She'd given herself until eleven o'clock to get the stick out of her ass and strike up a conversation with somebody, or just leave. No use sticking around until midnight when she didn't even have mice, a pumpkin, and glass slippers to worry about.

And all of a sudden, her fairy godmother of BDSM had gotten a huge damn clue.

And delivered a prince who defied her wildest, kinkiest dreams.

And *not* because he instantly reminded her of Dan.

Get off the Colton crazy train! Especially now!

It was his hair. It looked so much like Dan's dark blond waves, she was initially captivated—though her perception was likely hindered by the thick velvet strings from his mask, tossing all kinds of shadows through his thick style.

And about that mask…

Dear God.

Sometimes great minds really did think alike. Though it covered half his face and transformed his eyes into daunting mysteries, she tilted a little smile. She was *looking* for daunting, right?

She'd just had no idea how much. And one look at this man, powerful and beautiful and looming before her in nothing but his huge black boots, faded jeans, and that mask, revealed he probably had a doctorate in daunting.

She'd only concentrated on his covered parts so far, too. The face she couldn't quite decipher. The legs, endless and powerful, converging at a bulge beneath his zipper that stripped the moisture from her throat. But everything else was…

Dear God.

It bore repeating. Probably out loud. If she could only figure where the hell all her air had gone.

He was beautiful. Almost unreal. She'd only had this sensation a few times in her whole life, like the moment she'd gazed at her first Michelangelo statue in Rome, or gasped at a *Cirque* performer who supported three others in his palm. His lean but rock-hard build emphasized every captivating striation of his muscles: the hard ropes of his neck, the shoulders and arms that rivalled Red Rock for ridges, the abdomen that was another mountain range all on its own, as well. He moved a little closer to her with grace that reminded her of an eagle's flight, deadly force honed for efficiency and grace.

Was he even real?

She yearned to reach out and learn that answer for herself.

She'd never been more afraid to move in her life.

She cleared her throat. Tried to straighten her stance—but then wondered if she should lower her head, instead. Or bow. Or curtsy? Or shake his hand? *Hell.* She was the girl who'd read every damn research book on dungeon etiquette, right? But now she really did feel like the girl at the prom with toilet paper attached to her heel.

"Hi," she finally managed. "I—I mean hello. Hello, *Sir.* I—I mean—"

If she really *had* something to say after that, it would've have disappeared as soon as he lifted her hand between both of his and stepped closer, as if trying to figure her out more fully. His skin was firm and warm, his grip a steady command his eyes still impossible to read. "Ssshhh. Breathe, red."

Red. Though she liked playing up the unique color of her hair, she always cringed when someone used the too-typical nickname. But on his lips, the words were transformed into something new. Magical.

"Breathe. Right. Okay…*right.* God. I am so sorry. You must think I'm so—" She injected a weak laugh. "I'm normally better at the whole stringing-a-sentence-together thing, I promise."

Why was she blowing this so bad? And why did he make it worse with his disarming grin and his tightening hold? And the simple force of his presence. And the intensity of his nearness. And the potency of his scent. How could the combination of Scotch and dust suddenly smell so incredible?

"Why are you sorry? I'm the one who intruded."

"Oh, yeah. 'Intruded.'" She blew out a pseudo raspberry. "Because there was *so* much going on here in my corner to intrude on."

"There would have been." His mutter edged so close to an animal's timber, she shivered a little. Tess had listened to enough radio spy chatter over the years to know the small disc on his neck was a voice distorter of some sort, which should have raised her wariness—instead, it only added to his allure. Her pulse thrummed, a current strange yet wonderful. While she felt at once safe, she also knew she shouldn't…not this much, not this fast. The conflict only hastened to her reckless heartbeat, especially as he added, "Then I would've had to bounce a few skulls together."

"Why?" She knew how stupid it sounded. The possessive snarl beneath his words spoke enough meaning for anyone to figure out—except, perhaps, for her. The "protective" thing was usually *her* gig, a default when one was looking out for sisters who were "the pretty one" and "the smart ass," so grasping the concept that anyone wanted to look after her in the same way…

Weird. Very weird.

But ohhh…so nice.

Really nice.

Still, she braced herself for his teasing chuckle. Maybe some sarcastic quip at what a "silly subbie" she was for not comprehending his intent.

Once more, the man turned her expectations sideways. No. Fully upside-down. Her senses careened as he released a hand, lifting it to her jaw, yanking up her whole face for the focus of his fathomless gaze. "Why?" he repeated. "Because I'm pretty well set on having you all to myself tonight, rose." His fingers pressed in. "Unless you aren't interested in what you see?"

She laughed. She couldn't help herself. "You're kidding, right?"

"At the risk of being trite, do I look like I'm kidding?"

"At the risk of being obnoxious, do I look like a nun? Because that's the only situation I can imagine you being turned down, Sir Sexy."

Air pushed past his smirk. His thick stubble disguised the exact edges of his lips but the flash of his teeth briefly showed her that they were curved and lush…and maybe a little wicked.

Wicked. Right behind daunting on what she'd come here looking for.

"A WILDer Kind of Love – WILD Boys 7"
will be available on June 16, 2015

About Cherise Sinclair

Authors often say their characters argue with them.
Unfortunately, since Cherise Sinclair's heroes are Doms, she never, ever wins.

A *USA Today* Bestselling Author, Cherise is renowned for writing heart-wrenching romances with devastating Dominants, laugh-out-loud dialogue, and absolutely sizzling sex. And did I mention the BDSM? Her numerous awards include a National Leather Award, *Romantic Times* Reviewer's Choice nomination, and Best Author of the Year from the Goodreads BDSM group.

Fledglings having flown the nest, Cherise, her beloved husband, and one fussy feline live in the Pacific Northwest where nothing is cozier than a rainy day spent writing.

Connect with Cherise in the following places:

Website:
http://CheriseSinclair.com

Facebook:
www.facebook.com/CheriseSinclairAuthor

Facebook Discussion Group:
CheriseSinclair.com/Facebook-Discussion-Group

Want to be notified of the next release?

Sent only on release day, Cherise's newsletters contain freebies, excerpts, and articles.
Sign up at:
www.CheriseSinclair.com/NewsletterForm

Made in the USA
San Bernardino, CA
25 March 2016